Berringden

Sons and Lodgers

Jill Robinson

Berringden Books

For Tom Alex and Neil

And also Paul, Bob, Sehlile, Dunlop, Tom, Pat, Euan, Dikeledi, Sarah, Ros, Liz S., Ruth, Laura, Roley, Liz R., Susan, Ray, Ken, Julian, Ross, Sally, Dave, Pat, Victor and Sasha, Carole and Martin plus dog, Jerry and Mary plus two dogs, Alex's friends in the attic, the vagrants in the shed, and anyone else who has ever stayed under my roof in Berringden Brow.

Thanks to Alan Sparkes and John Billingsley

Disclaimer: This is a work of fiction and the identification of any character portrayed with any living person should not be presumed.

Published by Berringden Books

Printed by Viking Press on 01706 818776

Email: jill@berringdenbrow.co.uk

ISBN 0-9546400-0-4

Chapter 1

It was the smell of chocolate that told me I was almost home.

Berringden station is next to a chocolate factory, and my first impression of the town when I arrived fifteen years ago had been the smell of Quality Street.

As a child, I lived in a small West Country town famous for its brewery, and therefore grew up accustomed to a pervasive smell of hops; but stepping off the train that first time, and sniffing the scented air, I had recognised the sweet confectionery aroma of Berringden as being much more welcoming.

The bus up to Berringden Brow, the hill-top village where I now live, is not due for twenty minutes, and rather than shiver at the bus stop in the autumn chill, I decide to wait in the library, which stays open until seven o'clock this evening.

"Back again, Jess? That research job didn't last very long," observes Ben the librarian, as I approach the counter. He is right, since the mental health project in Bristol on which I have been working for the past six months ran into difficulties, and my involvement with it has ended sooner than expected. It turned out that I was a researcher with very little research to do, since fewer people than anticipated could be recruited for the project.

I explain this to Ben, and add that now I am back, I would like to renew my Passport To Leisure, the invaluable document which permits half price swims and reduced ticket prices to concerts, and also allows local people to borrow videos and CDs from the library at a discounted price. Library staff can issue the Passports, and I offer Ben an old photograph for the purpose. This is much better than my previous one, since it actually does still look a little like me, rather than the zombie with the perm featured on the now-expired PTL.

Ben looks at my picture and smiles, not in admiration but with quiet mirth.

"Hmm, a picture of you seemingly as a teenager. Wherever did this come from? It looks as if it has been cut from a contact sheet, and not very well at that, there's too much border left on it."

Ben is correct, the photograph was taken to accompany an article I was asked to write ten years ago for the 'Guardian' newspaper, on the fascinating subject of debt counselling. I was actually in my thirties then, but I suppose it is quite a flattering picture for someone middle aged (although obviously not nearly as glamorous as those photos taken of the mature Women's Institute ladies who posed naked behind their jam pans and ladles for a fund-raising calendar. Unfortunately, their part of Yorkshire is quite some distance from Berringden, so I can't join them. I would love to have seen Ben's face had I featured in the calendar, as say, Miss March, and had presented him with a picture from **that** contact sheet for inclusion in my Passport to Leisure.)

Ben shakes his head and sighs, bending over the application form, checking the details. I note that his dark hair shows no sign of thinning or going grey; but then, he is ten years my junior, and still on the right side of forty. How foolish I was last year to develop a crush on this younger, and as it turned out, unavailable man; still, all that is now over and done with; I am now happily reconciled to serene singleness, and freed of all emotional attachments, my life will hopefully be far less complicated than it has been recently…

At home, Alex greets me casually, as befits a cool teenager on seeing his mother finally returning after working away for six months.

"Hi Mum, had a good time? I'm off out with Kenny now, see you later. "

"Hold on, Alex; where are you going, and what time will you be back?"

"For a walk – with Kenny, I told you! Back for supper."

And so he disappears, leaving me to survey the chaos which is my home.

Of course, I have been back at weekends, and spent the time cleaning the house, doing mountains of washing and undertaking massive shopping expeditions to replenish the food cupboards. It almost appears that Alex and Nick, my friend and lodger, have not taken out the rubbish since I left in the Spring, they have just piled items up beside the overflowing bins. Now it is October. I used to complain about this, but it did no good at all, since Alex and Nick would profess in surprised tones that they had not realised I had wanted the bins emptying, I had not put it on the list of tasks. So each time I rewrote the list of tasks it grew longer and more detailed; (wash up dishes, take out rubbish, feed cat, do laundry, Hoover, clean loo, put out milk bottles, water plants, sweep kitchen floor etc,) so that in the end they could not be bothered to read it at all and blithely ignored the list altogether.

Now, there is a sink full of dirty dishes, and a trail of filthy pots and pans extends across every visible surface. Nutty the cat appears, looking lean and hungry, but there is no cat food in the cupboards, so I open a tin of pilchards. The houseplants are dying for lack of water, and the front room looks as if Alex has had a party, with discarded cigarette packets and empty beer cans and bottles of alcopops strewn around. The carpet is stained with food, drink, and what I hope is only mud. A picture has fallen off the wall and landed on the couch – I pick it up and gaze wistfully at the smiling faces of two good-looking boys, aged five and eleven, a school photograph of Alex and his elder brother Tom taken at junior school, when Tom was in the top class and Alex in reception. How long ago that now seems. Tom has been away at university for three years, and the delightful child who was once Alex has now turned into a stroppy teenager.

I venture into the garden, which in the evening twilight appears sorry and neglected and has a number of plastic bottles lying in the flower-beds. The fence has been demolished at the corner of the garden and the lock of the shed door has been broken. Peering cautiously inside, I realise with horror that someone has been sleeping rough, as there is a pile of tatty bedding and more old discarded bottles and tab ends. So much for the 'on-your-bike' theory of job search. I went to Bristol because I was offered a temporary job there, but now I wish I had stayed at home to look after the house and gone on the dole. The dilemma of single-parenthood is almost impossible to resolve; either spend time with the family and have no money - or work, earn, commute, pay travel and childcare expenses, probably exhaust yourself, and run the risk of neglecting the children. It is simply impossible to do two jobs effectively at once. These so-called super-women who appear to manage this feat must all have reliable help in the home, whereas I have only Nick, of whom there is at present no sign. Nick, who has been nominally in charge while I have been away, works late hours at the advice centre he runs, and then goes to do home visits and eat curry with housebound and disabled clients. What a homecoming this has turned out to be - enough to make me wish I had stayed longer in the library.

Nick appears just before midnight, carrying a fragrant parcel.

"I've brought you some supper", he says, unwrapping the remains of a few kebabs and samosas. I thank him and explain that Alex and I have had fish and chips five hours ago, since there was nothing to eat in the house except the tin of pilchards, and Nutty's need was greater than ours. Alex has not finished his chips, he did not seem very hungry, which surprised me after his walk; in fact he looked distinctly unwell and went to bed early. I hope he is not sickening for something.

"How are things at the Advice Centre?" I ask Nick. He too looks washed out, no doubt as a result of the very long hours. One of the many advantages of me returning to Berringden Brow is that I will be able to help Nick at the Centre, which is now properly funded. Nick set it up at Easter with his redundancy money and his betting shop winnings, which are often fairly considerable when he is on a winning streak, but which can hardly be said to form a secure basis for long-term funding. Now the Advice Centre has been properly registered as a charitable company limited by guarantee, and a philanthropic organisation has provided a three-year grant, so that payment of the rent, rates and running costs no longer has to depend on the outcome of the 3.30 at Chepstow.

Sometimes grateful clients give donations, but these are very often in kind, such as tonight's curry, rather than cash. Nick has also received a shalwar kamise, two pairs of ornate sandals in the wrong size, jars of coffee, various sweetmeats and countless packets of biscuits. He has also been offered free accommodation in Kashmir, should he ever choose to go there. However, thanks to the secure funding, he can now be paid a proper salary, and need not rely on this barter and exchange system, although I hear that something similar is all the rage in some places such as nearby Hebden Bridge, where a scheme operates along the lines of a glorified baby-sitting circle, with people exchanging 'favours' for various services rendered.

Alex is sick the next morning but it is half term, so he can stay in bed and recover. By lunch-time he seems fine, and says he wants to go for another walk with Kenny. I am mystified by this sudden interest in walking.

"Where do you go on these walks?"

"Oh, around and about," says Alex. "Up the Berringden Valley to the reservoirs at the top. I thought you would be pleased we're doing something healthy, going on these nature rambles, getting fresh air and exercise."

I tell him I am – if indeed that's all he is getting. It seems so out of character, and I am starting to have my suspicions. I pay an early visit to the library, and head for the Natural Science section. I am looking at a book on fungi when Ben comes by with a trolleyful of recent returns, and peers over my shoulder.

"Revisiting your hippy past?"

"Discovering my son's criminal present," I reply grimly, since it appears that magic mushrooms, known to grow well in the Berringden area, count as class A drugs, and Alex displays many of the symptoms associated with their use. I shall have to have strong words with that lad – and pray for an early frost.

Chapter 2

St. Mary's, our local parish church, is holding a Barn Dance to raise funds, so I buy two tickets and invite Frank. Following our unsatisfactory affair last year, during which I had unsuccessfully attempted to rescue the 50 year old Frank from the clutches of the elderly mother with whom he still lives, we have reverted to our previous arrangement of being simply Barn Dance partners. After a long spell of unemployment, Frank has been dragooned onto yet another government employment scheme, and is currently running a leisure centre in his home village in run-down South Yorkshire. I tease him about this, likening his situation to the "Brittas Empire" TV sitcom, similarly set in a sports centre and presided over by an officious chap in some ways not unlike Frank.

Since we gave up any attempt at closeness, Frank has reclassified me in the role of agony aunt, and takes care to give me up-to-date news about his love-life, or lack of it, despite the fact that I am really not at all interested. He has enrolled with an internet dating group, but tells me that all the women featured 'look like dogs.' I tell him crossly that they are probably very nice people when you get to know them, and anyway, in such matters you should not go on looks (especially not as shown in those dreadful little passport photos) but on personality and common interests. Nothing annoys me more than 'lookist' men, and I try to practise what I preach and not to judge a book by its cover, so to speak; but I have to say, Frank himself is no oil painting. (You can always tell when I am angry, because I start spouting clichés.) At least we still have the barn dancing in common, and it must be said that he is a very good dancer, always remembering the moves and knowing the correct way to turn.

The dance is to be held in the school next-door to where I live. When Frank and I arrive, most of the parishioners are sitting glumly round the room, unsure as to why they are here, and looking for all the world as if they would much have preferred to stay home and watch 'Blind Date.' The beleaguered caller is vainly trying to encourage couples to get to their feet to make up a square set for the first dance.

"Come on, girl," says Frank. "We had better show them how it's done."

He leads me onto the floor, and we stand there alone facing the band. A few more of the would-be dancers reluctantly follow. There are still more wall-flowers than dancers, however; people seem to be afraid of making fools of themselves, and provide a variety of excuses for not dancing - bad feet, bad legs, bad balance, bad breath, (well, breathlessness actually.) People claim to be unable to dance, confess themselves unwilling to dance, or to have no sense of timing; they announce that they possess two left feet, or have come incorrectly attired, in tight skirts or shoes that pinch. They have bought tickets in order to support the church, but plan to escape as soon as decently possible after the pie and pea supper interval. The event is definitely regarded by many as something of a penance rather than as an evening to be enjoyed, indeed, I feel that some would prefer to go on a pilgrimage on their knees, rather than attempt a 'Strip the willow'. The revelation that Frank and I go Barn Dancing every month voluntarily is greeted with astonishment.

"Your friend is very good, isn't he," says Sarah, during the break. Frank is in his element tonight, as we have ended up sharing a supper table with two young women, both unaccompanied single parents. I chat with Sarah, asking her about her recent house move, but Frank has eyes only for Suzanne, with her pretty face, blond hair and lovely figure. He gazes, full of undisguised admiration, as Suzanne returns to the table with her pie and peas, her skin-tight jeans and high-heeled boots showing off her elegant legs, and a figure-hugging sweater emphasising the rest of her charms. Frank is so deeply smitten that he sits out the next two dances in order to be able to continue his conversation with Suzanne, who is not dancing. Meanwhile, I grab Jim the vicar for the 'Nottingham swing'. Then I do a hectic 'Cumberland Square' with Jeremy the churchwarden. Eventually, Frank tears himself away from Suzanne, having asked her three times if she will dance and being smilingly refused, and takes me back onto the floor. He looks down at me, and begins to tut-tut and frown.

"You'd really better start dyeing your hair, Jess, it's getting quite grey. It'll soon be like dancing with a badger..."

The caller announces another square dance, the first movement of which is to step-balance on the corner. My corner person is Alastair, my solicitor, but unfortunately setting off on the wrong foot, we succeed only in kicking each other's shins. As we exchange rueful grimaces, I hope he will not sue me for inadvertent actual bodily harm. The moves become increasingly confusing.

"Dosey-do your opposite, then chain for three and Box the Gnat!" shouts the caller. "Set and Gypsy. Chain back and Box the Flea – no, that's to your **left**"

"And people complain about legal jargon" observes Alastair.

As we make our way back to my house, Frank is still in a daze about Suzanne, whose two teenage sons have arrived to escort her home.

"Why on earth is she on her own? She has an absolutely gorgeous figure, and her face isn't bad either. Surely she could find someone; in fact, I was just about to ask her out myself when those lads turned up. We were getting on really well. You don't have her phone number, I suppose do you Jess? Is she in the book – what's her surname? And that girl you were talking to – what was her name? Sarah - she wasn't bad-looking either, only she's very skinny, and of course, skinny women don't really attract me, as you know."

I tell Frank to shut up, or he will also receive a kick on the shins; only in this case the defence will be unable to claim that it was inadvertent. It is useless me telling him that Suzanne does not live alone, she has her two teenage sons with her; and perhaps she prefers to be without a male partner – many women do, it is peaceful, no-one compares our appearance to dogs or badgers, and we can please ourselves. Frank simply does not accept such arguments. What woman would choose to be without a man, if there were one available, seems to be his line of thinking. This is why I fell out with Frank – he is unable to meet, or even see a woman in the street, without embarking on a critique of her face and form, or to begin pondering over the whys and wherefores of her domestic situation. He assures me that all men think the thoughts he speaks aloud, even if they do not care to admit it. I do not know if this is true; but at least the majority of the men I know have the decency to keep such opinions to themselves when in mixed company.

Chapter 3

"What about these mushrooms, Alex? I know that's why you have developed this sudden interest in walking."

Alex keeps cool. "Well, Mum, you were always taking us out on nature rambles when we were younger to pick free food – bilberries and blackberries and field mushrooms and stuff, so you mustn't be surprised if I do the same."

"I never encouraged you to pick Class A drugs, Alex!"

"Class A drugs! What on earth are you on about? Mushies are a natural product."

I fetch the library book and thrust it under Alex's nose. "Well that book's wrong, it's out of date Mum. Mushies are harmless."

"They make you sick, and this book was only published last year."

Alex looks out of the window. "Well, it doesn't matter now, because there's been a frost, that's it for this season. Mum, can I have a sleep-over tonight?" Alex is obviously keen to change the subject, but I am reluctant to grant his request, recalling a previous occasion when all house rules relating to drink, cigarettes and pornography had been broken. However, Alex tells me impatiently that this present sleep-over was arranged while I was still away, and a different set of boys are coming this time, nice well-behaved ones.

"And at least you will know where I am – I'll be here, not walking about on the hills," he adds in a final attempt to win me over. I reluctantly give my consent.

Later on, three boys arrive carrying sleeping bags and rucksacks, and are ushered upstairs to Tom's room, which serves as our guest quarters now that the rightful occupant lives in Bristol. The boys settle down, lying in their sleeping bags, chattering and watching TV. I pop in at 11 o'clock, to make sure they have everything they need by way of cushions and blankets. All appears to be well, so I bid them goodnight, then retire to the living room to watch "Late Review". I fall asleep during the programme, despite the fact that Tom Paulin is one of this week's guest reviewers, and wake up with a start at midnight, feeling cold. Going upstairs to the bathroom, I sense that it is unusually quiet – I can hear none of the muffled giggles and snores usually associated with teenage sleepovers. Putting my head round the bedroom door, my suspicions are confirmed – all four boys have gone.

It is an extremely cold October night, and I shiver as I rush into the garden in my slippers, calling for Alex, but there is no reply. I put on shoes and coat, and seizing a torch, I run around the estate, calling and calling, but still no answer. I spend the next forty minutes searching round the village, but there is no sign of anyone. All is calm and cold. My voice echoes across the Berringden valley, thin and forlorn.

I curse the fact that I no longer have a car, so cannot drive up to Midgley, as the recreation ground there is one of Alex's favourite haunts. But would he be up there on a night like this? I do not feel I want to climb the steep, lonely footpath that leads up to Midgley rec on my own at dead of frosty night. There seems to be no option but to call the police. They sound less than thrilled at the prospect of having to turn out to look for four lads, but on hearing that the boys are aged fifteen, they reluctantly drive round the village in the Panda car, and return shaking their heads. "It's brass monkeys tonight; no way are those little beggars going to be out in this weather, they'll be safely tucked up in someone's house watching videos."

"But where?" I can't think of any child whose parents are away, and it is hardly likely that any sane adult will welcome four teenagers clattering in at midnight. "I'm sure they are out there somewhere – did you try Midgley rec?" But the policemen say they are fed up with touring the locality and want to return to the police station for bacon and eggs.

"Well, if you cannot do any more, then what about the police helicopter?"

The policemen assure me that this can only be scrambled at great expense, to which I reply that that is why I pay my rates. By now I am imagining the worst, the boys will have fallen prey to unsavoury characters in public toilets, until I remember that all the local conveniences have been closed by the council as a cost-cutting measure, so people have to wee in hedge bottoms, which is probably where the unsavoury characters now sleep. To appease me, in my increasingly agitated state, the policemen agree to call out the helicopter, and disappear to eat their delayed midnight fry-up.

The sound of the helicopter, clattering over the opposite hillside, its searchlights systematically sweeping from side to side, distracts me. There will be no hiding place for those lads out of doors anywhere in Berringden Brow. Despite the police assurance that the exercise is a complete waste of time, I sense that Alex and his friends are out there somewhere. And soon it is apparent that I am right – what mother is not? Ten minutes later, the Panda car returns, having been radioed by the helicopter, when almost within bacon-sandwich smelling distance of the Police Station, with the news that the boys are indeed up at Midgley rec. The disgruntled officers have been obliged to turn the car round and go to retrieve the unhappy and extremely ill lads.

Alex is violently sick as he reaches the front door, while Nigel can hardly stagger down the path before collapsing in the hall. Josh does not appear to be quite as bad, but is moaning and saying his head hurts. However, most alarming of all is the absence of Dick– he has apparently run off at the sight of the Panda car, and is now out in the cold all by his drunken self, perhaps at this very moment choking or even asphyxiating. The police refuse to look for him again, saying that as they have found him once, and he has legged it, they have no duty to prolong the search.

I telephone the other parents and ask them to collect their sons; it is dreadful to have to admit what has happened, what with the noise of groaning and vomiting going on in the background. "Whatever sort of household is this?" enquires Nigel's father icily, as he retrieves his son, while Josh's mother says that her Josh has never done anything like this before, and would never even think of such a thing, so Alex must have put him up to it. Dick's mother Rachel is the most understanding, and she immediately drives off to search the local highways and byways. The police then start to tick me off, saying that the boys were not properly supervised, but surely people cannot be expected to keep an all-night vigil beside fifteen-year olds? And where did they get the booze? In between bouts of sickness, Alex explains that the others had called at the off-licence on their way, and prevailed upon an unknown man to buy cheap cider, the rocket fuel sort that comes in plastic bottles. They had paid him out of their paper-round earnings, and smuggled the bottles into my house inside the sleeping bags. That old trick! I should have known better.

The whole thing had been planned last week at school, and was not the first time, as they had got away with it successfully during the summer holidays when camping in Dick's back garden, well out of earshot of the house.

The police finally depart at three a.m. saying they will have a word with the proprietor of the off-licence, who perhaps ought to be suspicious when someone buys huge amounts of the cheapest cider, as no-one but under-age lads ever drinks the stuff. I clean Alex up and put him to bed, with a bucket to hand, and retire to my room. However, I cannot sleep, for worrying about Dick, perhaps lying dead under a hedge, as it is still bitterly cold, and drunken people can easily succumb to hypothermia. I imagine an inquest, and all our photographs in the local paper, under headlines such as "Misadventure at Midgley", "Recklessness in the rec," "Half-term Hi-jinks end in tragedy," or worst of all "Berringden Brow boy in dawn death discovery." Then I hear the five o'clock clatter of milk bottles, and rush down to tell the tale to Bella the milk lady, asking her to keep a look-out for Dick on her rounds. I would trust her ability to find a missing lad over that of the police any day.

Finally, the phone rings at 7.30; it is Rachel, saying that Dick has just walked in. Having run away at the sight of the police, he was sick, fell asleep in a bush, then woke up feeling much better, although very cold. Luckily, Dick is fairly plump, and was wearing a thick jumper and padded coat - of the four boys, he was the most warmly dressed. Being completely disoriented, he had then walked round until he found himself passing my house. If only he had knocked on the door he could have saved us hours of worry. He had then made his way home across the fields, unaware that his mother was driving up and down the roads searching for him.

So all has ended well, except – the police have me down as a bad mother; the other parents think that I preside over a disreputable household; the police helicopter has been scrambled at vast expense to the Berringden ratepayers; four boys have made themselves sick with cider and their parents sick with worry; and yet again Alex has betrayed my trust. Perhaps I should try to get him into some sort of approved school or Borstal - don't they call them 'boot camps' these days - if any such institutions exist locally. Or have they suffered the same fate as the Berringden Brow public toilets, and been closed down? I know we all have to look out for ourselves these days, there is no such thing as society, and people bemoan the lack of community spirit. However, without a partner, extended family or any great financial resources, I am obliged to admit that I am finding the task of bringing up Alex a real struggle.

Chapter 4

Nick and I have been invited to the wedding of an old friend, Don Hesketh, and his Filipino bride, Cory, whom he met when he and Nick were on holiday in Singapore. Cory was a friend of Hesketh's cousin's housemaid, and there had been talk of her finding another lady for Nick, but this had not worked out, (perhaps just as well, since Nick's mother may not have been too keen on him importing an Asian bride.) Nick has recently returned to his mother's house, for a change of scene and a period of recuperation after house- and Alex-sitting for me for six months. He migrates from one abode to the other with the seasons, as his mother's house is warmer than mine in winter, yet the hill-side estate where I live is within walking distance of his advice centre, so he returns to me in the Spring, rather like the cuckoos. " April come he will…"etc.

I recall the time, years ago, when Nick, Hesketh and I were all working at Berringden Citizens' Advice Bureau, and had gone on holiday together. I had foolishly agreed to share a large room with three single beds, in an attempt to keep costs down. I figured that I could get changed in the en suite bathroom, and thought the arrangement should work out OK, but of course, it didn't. As soon as we arrived, Nick and Hesketh headed off to the bars and bright lights, leaving me to spend a quiet evening strolling along the beach, all by myself in the moonlight, before retiring early. The problem was that there was only one key for the room, which I had kept; and as I did not want to have to get up in the middle of the night to let the others back in, I left the door slightly ajar, wedged with a piece of card, so it would not slam shut.

I was awakened at four in the morning by the sound of Hesketh falling through the door in a drunken stupor. Picking himself up, he flopped onto his bed.

"Where's Nick?" I asked anxiously.

"Oh, I dunnow; he went off with shome woman," replied Hesketh thickly. He then fell noisily asleep, and I knew I would not be able to get any sense out of him. I tried to doze, but forgot to ensure that the door was still wedged open, as of course it had slammed shut behind Hesketh. At five o'clock I heard the sound of an altercation in the corridor. I got up and found Nick outside the door, in drunken conversation with an aggrieved taxi-driver. As soon as he realised the door was open, Nick scuttled into the room, leaving me to face the irate cabbie. It appeared that he had brought Hesketh back an hour earlier, and had been told to wait while his passenger fetched the money for the fare. Hesketh had promptly run off, pursued by the taxi-driver, through the labyrinth of hotel corridors, with several dead ends and blind alleys leading to closets and cupboards, and it had taken him an hour to locate the correct room. Naturally, I did not wish to pay Hesketh's taxi fare, and I knew there was no chance of arousing him from his drunken slumbers, so I advised the cabbie to return later in the day, when Hesketh might have sobered up.

Meanwhile, I could hear Nick being violently ill in the bathroom. He presented a bizarre appearance, wild-eyed and ashen-faced, his cheeks streaked with vivid red lipstick. His clothes were in complete disarray, with the shirt buttoned up in a lop-sided fashion; and as he removed his trousers, which were already at half-mast, it became apparent that his underpants were on back to front. To complete the spectacle, a condom had fallen onto the floor. I decided to leave him to it and returned to bed yet again, but I was unable to sleep. In contrast, both chaps were soon slumbering soundly. Why on earth had I agreed to come on holiday with these two? I must be utterly mad not to have insisted on a single room, never mind the expense. And we were all supposed to be respectable advice workers, in our thirties, not a bunch of teenagers let loose on a first trip to some party island location without parental supervision.

However, it seems that the effect of being abroad does turn Nick into something of an adolescent, as I recalled a similar scenario in Zimbabwe a few years earlier, when Nick had spent the night in a tin hut in the township at Victoria Falls with a local lady. Meanwhile, I had passed sleepless hours of worry in our tent with Alex at the campsite, concerned that Nick might have been mugged or fallen into the Zambezi. So enamoured of the young woman was he that he had spent the rest of the holiday with her, (plus various member of her extended family, who soon heard that there was a rich and gullible Englishman in town), in the local bars and discos. Meanwhile, Alex and I did the more traditional tourist things, such as hiring bikes, viewing the Falls, going round the nature reserve and visiting the crocodile farm. The young lady's family had suggested that Nick remain there and marry her, but he had, at the last minute, decided to return with Alex and me on the train to Bulawayo. The relatives had brought him back to the campsite, just as Alex and I had finished packing up the tent and were about to leave for the station. I had, quite understandably in the circumstances, given Nick a piece of my mind, which shocked the young lady's family, so much so that one of them had asked Alex if I was Nick's wife – it seemed that only a wife could possibly be that cross with him. Nick had apparently neglected to mention to his new friends that he was travelling with a woman and child. I had vowed at the time never to go on holiday with Nick again, but had foolishly broken this promise to myself and was yet again reaping the consequences.

The following morning, Nick could be heard rummaging in his bag, moaning.

"Oh, f…, she's taken it all".

"Surely you didn't take all your money out with you last night?" I asked.

"Well, I can't remember what I did take; and I can't find my English money now…" I seized Nick's bag, and turned out all the pockets.

"The English money's here; she could only have taken the local currency."

At this, Nick cheered up, as he worked out that this could only have been worth about seventeen pounds. Still, quite an expensive mistake, as he had already paid her the fee required for her services. Nick explained that having gone off with one woman to her room, he had no idea of how to get back to the hotel after she had finished with him. Blundering around in the back streets, he had come across another woman, and this one had her mother with her. He had attempted to ask them for directions, but they had seen him coming and carted him off up a dark alley. When he eventually was able to make his escape, he ran into a couple of men, who luckily took pity on him rather than taking advantage. Nick had no idea of the name of our hotel, but knew it was on the sea-front, so his saviours marched him all the way along until he finally recognised the hotel, right at the end of the promenade.

The taxi-driver reappeared, and the now sober Hesketh went out with the fare and an apology. This holiday was going to be very tiring if the men were going to persist in getting into these kinds of scrapes. I asked the hotel staff if there was a single room I could have, but there was none available, so I had no choice but to make the best of it. Nick and Hesketh promised to be more considerate and return quietly after their nocturnal escapades. Unsurprisingly, everyone was very tired the following evening, and we all had an early night.

Now Hesketh is marrying his Filipino sweetheart, so hopefully he will settle down and put all such adventures behind him. He and Cory leave the Register Office and pause on the steps for the photographs. Then I spot two familiar figures lurking in the rhododendron bushes, trying to look unobtrusive - Nick's mum and his Aunt Marigold, neither of whom can resist a wedding.

"And when can we expect to see you getting married, Nick? Haven't you met any nice young ladies?" asks Aunt Marigold.

Nick giggles by way of reply. I don't dare say anything. If only she knew.

Chapter 5

I spot my elderly neighbour, Wilf, swaying about in the precinct outside the market, one lunchtime. He is haranguing a couple whose glazed expressions appear to indicate that they are anxious to get away. Luckily for them, Wilf sees me and beckons me over, so the couple take the opportunity to escape.

"Come and have a drink with me, lovey. Tell me what tha's up to these days. Are you working? Are you courting? Hey, I heard in the shop that the Police helicopter was out searching for your Alex t'other neet - is that right?" I nod.

"Well, the little bugger needs his backside kicking. That's why you need a fella. Why can't you find one – you're young yet. If I wasn't with Myrtle, I'd have you."

"Thank goodness for Myrtle, then," I want to reply, but of course, I don't. Wilf is in his nineties, and drinking is his chief occupation. I suppose forty-something is young by his reckoning.

"Thanks, Wilf, but I don't want someone who's always in the pub. And I have to return to the Advice Centre before long. I'm working there, helping Nick."

Wilf looks disappointed and bends over me in a confidential manner. He is extremely tall, and has to stoop to whisper in my ear.

"Eh, I wanted you to come so I can tell you the news about my daughter. I'm worried, lass, she's not well. They say it's leukaemia."

Wilf is very proud of his daughter, a famous actress, well known for her film, television and stage roles. I tell him that I am very sorry to hear this news, and that I will call and visit him and Myrtle on my day off. This appears to satisfy Wilf, who totters off in the direction of the bus station. He will not catch the next bus, though, since he will probably run into at least half a dozen acquaintances between here and the bus stop. I'm sure he must know everyone in Berringden Brow.

I arrive home at teatime to discover Alex playing with a dog.

"Kenny and I were out on a walk – it's OK, there's no mushies left after the frost - and she followed us home," he explains. "Have you got any money, she's well hungry and she's already eaten the cat's food. We ought to get her some proper dog food."

"She's *very* hungry, not well," I automatically correct Alex. "But we ought to find out who she belongs to. Isn't there a name or number on her collar?"

"No, nothing. She's mine now. I'm calling her Brownie. Mum, she's a Staffie, what I've always wanted."

Alex has indeed always wanted a dog, but I have steadfastly resisted, as they are so demanding and expensive to keep, what with food and vets fees and injections. Also, I do not think Nutty, our geriatric cat, would appreciate a canine companion pestering her and eating her food. Besides, this dog must belong to someone, as she appears well kept, albeit hungry. Alex and I search in handbags and pockets, and copper up to buy dog food, managing to find 86 pence between us. Alex rushes off to the shop, returning with a tin, which Brownie immediately wolfs down. Meanwhile, I am on the phone to the local branch of the RSPCA. They inform me that a Miss Jones of Nether Berringden has reported her dog missing, so I phone this lady, with Alex protesting all the while. However, it turns out that Miss Jones's dog is a male, not a bitch, and he has actually returned home that afternoon.

As I relay this news to Alex, the phone rings. I answer, and a voice growls,

"Ah bleev you've got mi dog there. Is ee brindled with a docked tail?"

"No – and anyway, this one here's a bitch."

"Oh, well – in that case its mi friend's dog, 'ee's gone to Morecambe for a few days and left 'is dog out…"

"How irresponsible!" I put the phone down, wishing I had remembered to dial 141 before calling Miss Jones, who has evidently dialled 1471 to trace my number and given it to her friends. No doubt half the population of Nether Berringden will be phoning up, trying to con me out of this dog, as I know that Staffordshire Bull Terriers are very popular, especially in certain localities, and the bitches are valued for breeding. As if echoing my thoughts, the phone rings again.

"'Ave ya' got a brindled Staff there?"

"No, it's a sort of fawny beige colour, and anyway her owner has been traced."

Let's hope that puts a stop to these calls. I watch Brownie and Alex returning from a run up the road. Alex has her on a lead – where did that come from, I wonder.

"Alex, where did you get the dog's lead?"

"I found it in a hedge two years ago and kept it in case you ever relented and let me have a dog. Mum, she's weed and done a pooh, and it's getting dark, so she'd better stay here the night."

"OK, she can sleep in the shed."

Alex looks aghast. "No, it's much too cold in the shed! She'll sleep in my room. She can have that old sleeping bag."

Alex settles the dog on the sleeping bag in the corner of his room; but when I look in later, both Alex and Brownie are snuggled up together in bed fast asleep. Brownie looks very contented, and this is definitely the earliest Alex has been in bed since he was at Junior School.

The following morning there is no food for Brownie's breakfast, and I remember reading somewhere that cat-food is not good for dogs, so I give her some bread crusts soaked in Oxo, which she appears to find acceptable. The cat is looking very alarmed, and gives the capering Brownie a wide berth. Luckily it is Saturday, so I have the whole day to solve the dog dilemma. The next course of action seems to be to contact the Police. There has indeed been a lost dog reported, up by the Berringden reservoir. This is where Alex and Kenny had been walking. Alex's face clouds over at this news, but I am determined to reunite Brownie with her owner. Alex takes her for a walk while I telephone the number given me by the Police, remembering to preface it with 141. A man on the other end confirms that his son has lost his fawn-coloured female Staffie, Molly, and Brownie appears to fit the description. The son, Mike, will come straight away, bringing a photo to confirm that our Brownie is indeed his Molly.

"He's been lost without her," says the father. "He's either been out searching for her, or he's been moping round the house, daft as a brush; she's everything to him since his marriage broke up."

Alex is very upset to hear that Brownie's owner has been traced.

"But Alex, just imagine how you would feel if you lost a much-loved dog."

"I would have had my much-loved dog micro-chipped and wearing an identity tag on her collar."

This is indeed a fair point. When middle-aged Mike arrives, Brownie seems pleased to see him, but not overjoyed. She does not appear to be desperate to leave our house, and seems to think she is on holiday. Mike produces a picture of Molly, from which there can be no doubt of Brownie's true identity. As Alex rushes out in tears, I feel it is my maternal duty to tear Mike off a strip.

"You know, Mike, you could have saved yourself all this heartache, and Alex all this upset, not to mention me a great deal of time and trouble, if Molly only had some means of identification. Why don't you get her collar engraved?"

Mike mutters something about meaning to get it done.

"Well, make it a priority. You're very lucky to get her back; I had all sorts of strange people ringing me up last night, wanting to take Molly away. Not everyone would have gone to all this trouble to find her owner, they might easily have decided to keep her, and who could blame them?"

Mike looks uneasy, but I continue my tirade. "I don't know if you are planning to let Molly have any pups, but if you ever do, I think you owe Alex a dog."

Mike nods, and says that he is hoping that Molly will have a litter in the Spring.

I insist that he takes our phone number and notifies us immediately should there be a canine happy event. He and Molly leave, and it is not until their van turns the corner that Alex returns, and rushes, still red-eyed, to his room.

Chapter 6

It is my day off, and I remember that I promised to visit Wilf and Myrtle. As I reach the block of flats where they live, I notice a taxi-driver attempting to decant a passenger from his cab. It is Wilf, incoherently babbling abuse at the poor driver. Wilf falls out of the taxi and lies sprawling on the grass, complete with waving walking stick, six foot three of nonagenarian drunkenness. I shudder, wishing I had chosen a different time for my visit.

"He hasn't paid me, " complains the driver.

"Come on Wilf, put your hand in your pocket and pay the man," I entreat. Wilf mutters about the fare having gone up by fifty pence.

"Well, even if it has, you'll just have to pay up. Shall I fetch Myrtle?"

"No, not Myrtle," Wilf, still lying on the grass, manages to find his money and gives the driver a handful of coins. The driver makes as if to leave.

"Wait!! Can't you help me get him to his feet?" I entreat the departing cabbie.

"Sorry, lady – I have to pick up another fare. You really need an ambulance, not a taxi."

I know Myrtle will be unable to help me lift Wilf, since she is less than five foot tall, very frail and arthritic. I am about to call out the ambulance service on my mobile phone when Alex and Kenny appear.

"Ah lads, am I glad to see you! Help me get Wilf up to the second floor."

Alex and Kenny are strapping teenagers, but even they experience difficulty trying to lift a gangling, uncooperative ninety-something year-old, whose walking stick is flailing about, and who is continuing to mutter complaints about the fare increase, even though the taxi-driver is no longer in earshot. It does not help that the lads are chortling with laughter all the while.

"Heck, he's proper plastered, " says Alex.

"Yea, well inebriated," Kenny agrees. They loop Wilf's arms over their shoulders and drag him to the door. Of course, there is a recently-installed entry-phone system, and I cannot remember the correct number of Wilf's flat. Neither can he. I resort to calling up all the flats on the second floor until, at the third try, Myrtle answers. She releases the door, and the boys drag Wilf to the lift. At this point, Wilf sobers up sufficiently to tell us that the lift is not working, so they are obliged to drag him up two flights of concrete stairs, with me pushing from behind. It is not easy, and twice he almost falls back down the steps. Myrtle appears on the landing, and at the sight of her, Wilf breaks down and sobs his apologies. Myrtle comforts him, as the boys propel him through the door and onto a sofa in the living room. The boys and I attempt our escape, but Wilf is now getting maudlin, and grasping my arm, he announces that he wants to kiss me. However, I do not want to be kissed, and recoil from his beery breath and whiskery face.

"It's his daughter," Myrtle explains. "She's really poorly. It's only a matter of time now, the doctors say." Well, if Wilf really needs an excuse to get disgracefully drunk, then I have to admit that receiving news of the terminal illness of a beloved daughter appears to be as good as any.

Frank calls to tell me he has been asked to write a spoof Mummers play for the forthcoming New Year celebrations, to be performed at the country dance club he attends. The only trouble is he can't think what to write. The traditional form of the Mummers play was to have performers blacked up or in disguise, representing various characters, including the forces of good and evil. The plays were often in verse. Frank wants his play to be topical, and thinks the main character could be someone called Phoney Tony. Well of course, his opposite number should be Little Willie, "remember, that while I'm around, we'll never lose the British pound"; and what about Piers No'more, "in days of yore, he sat in judgement on the law; but now, alas he's been thrown out, so has to sit and nurse his gout", an abolished member of the House of Lords? You get the general idea.

Frank and I sit round my kitchen table one wet Sunday afternoon, and write a ten minute sketch, the villain of course being Millennium Bug and the hero an IT technician. Later, I hear a radio announcement that the Blairs are expecting a baby, so have to quickly add a character, rather unoriginally called Cherie – "Oh Tony, I've had such a shock, for I've just been to see the doc. He says I'm pregnant once again – there'll be a babe in Number 10", at which Phoney Tony exclaims "Not even Mandelson could dream up such a cunning clever scheme for focusing all media attention - no other news will get a mention! My dear Cherie, you are the best; now run along and get some rest."

Frank reads through the draft script while I make a cup of tea, his with goats milk because of his irritable bowel syndrome which means he has to be very careful with dairy products. There are so many things he 'can't touch.'

"You're not bad at this play-writing," he comments.

"Despite the fact my hair is going grey," I reply, pouring the tea.

I go to the library next day to look up some information on Mummers plays. Ben is looking tired and distracted. Maybe he had a bad weekend? I ask him about Mummers plays and he directs me upstairs to the reference section, where his partner, Lesley works. She helps me find a book about Mummers plays in the local collection; there are several versions still performed in the Berringden Valley. The main problem will be getting the members of the country dance club to remember their lines on Millennium night; goodness knows how we are going to achieve that.

I really must do something about the garden. I have tacked the damaged fence panel back up, but whoever it is that comes into the garden from the back lane has broken it down again. I also put a new padlock on the shed door, but that too has been forced. And the garden is always full of those plastic bottles – if I pick them up and put them in the dustbin, I find the next day that the have been retrieved and are again lying on the lawn. I ask the crime prevention officer for advice, but he says it is up to me to secure my own property. I cannot afford a new fence, and I really don't know what to do, except try to sell the house and move to a yob-free location, should there happen to be any such place locally within my means, which I doubt.

Chapter 7

Alex and I arrive in Bristol for Tom's graduation ceremony. I have borrowed an old Fiat Panda from one of Nick's clients, who operates a used-car business out of his back yard; it goes quite well, and we arrive early. Tom's father, Bill has also travelled down from his home in Selby. Tom is sharing a house with five others and it is all rather chaotic, with last-minute searches for the iron followed by hurried pressing of shirts, but at last we are ready to go to the Cathedral, where the degree conferment ceremony is to be held. It is a fine autumn day, and Tom is wearing a smart, but short-sleeved black shirt. I assume he has a jacket in his father's car. When we arrive, Tom goes to the cloisters to find his robes, and reappears looking very odd. His bare arms are sticking out from the sleeves of the gown rather like turkey drumsticks.

"Tom, where's your jacket?" I ask.

Tom looks non-plussed. "It's such a nice day I didn't think I would need one."

"But your arms! You've got goose-bumps."

It is much cooler in the cathedral than outside in the sunshine, and Alex is still wearing his fleece coat.

Bill groans. "Well, Tom, looks like we'll have to go all the way back to the house to collect a jacket, as you can't appear like that."

"But we don't have time!" I try not to shriek. Then I come up with a solution. Removing my own jacket, (black, bought for one pound fifty from the parish Pop-In shop some years ago, but still quite serviceable), I hand it to Tom.

"Mum, I can't wear this!"

"Yes you can! The only bit that will show from under the gown is the sleeves."

Tom puts the jacket on with the gown on top, and the problem is solved. It somehow reminds me of the old days when both the boys were young and always falling into streams or cowpats; so that we always had to take a spare set of clothes with us wherever we went. The classic case was when Alex arrived somewhere one winter's day and thought the icy patch outside the building would be fine to slide on. The only trouble was, the ice was simply a thin film on the surface of a pond, and he was plunged into freezing water up to his waist. Alex was then very grateful for an old pair of jogging bottoms, found in the boot of the car, which normally he would not have been seen dead in, just as Tom is never again likely to contemplate wearing my Pop-In shop jacket. The trouble is that I am now jacketless and feeling cold in my thin blouse; but never mind, it is not me having my degree conferred in a blaze of flash-lights and camcorders. By this time, nearly all the seats have been taken, so Alex, Bill and I make out way to the back row, where I can stand shivering, quietly unobserved. And even if I am the chilliest mother in the entire congregation, I feel I am possibly also the proudest.

Afterwards, Tom and all his friends throw their hats into the air for the traditional photograph, and I warm up in the sunshine on College Green, while Bill enjoys a surreptitious cigarette and Alex tries on a mortar-board he has found on the grass. A large family approaches me and someone asks if I will take a picture of all of them, but, try as I will, I cannot get their camera to work.

"Just press the red button!" they exhort, clicking their tongues and shaking their heads at my incompetence. Eventually one of them comes over to check what it can possibly be that I am doing wrong, and realises that the film has finished. I am extremely relieved that it is not my stupidity after all.

That evening, the four of us go for a meal at a Chilean restaurant just off the Gloucester Road, this is Tom's choice, it is his day. I suddenly realise that I have been here before, years ago, with Robin, my former partner, now teaching in Botswana. He and I visited some Trade Union friends of his in Bristol and went to a fund-raising dinner for some Latin America good cause in this very restaurant – Cuban schools, I think. In fact, I even have a few photographs of the occasion somewhere at home. It seems strange, being here again without Robin. I am on the very periphery of his life now, when once, at the time when we visited this restaurant, I was so central to it. It is different with Bill; of course, I am now marginal to his life, too; but we have Tom, and can still associate amicably on occasions such as today. And I quite often ring his partner, Chris, for a chat, we have become good friends, whereas of course this does not apply to Tebogo, Robin's African lady-friend.

The meal is delicious, and we tuck in, suddenly hungry after our long day. Bill and I share the cost between us, then take Tom back to his house, as he has to go to work the next day. Tom has a job at the off-licence round the corner, in fact it is the same work he was doing during his student days. He seems to enjoy it, although of course he is applying for proper professional jobs all the time. In Tom's shared household of six, only one, Rose, has obtained work in keeping with her degree, as she has a job in publishing. The others are working in fast-food retailing or for temping agencies. (Hence that old joke – 'What do you say to a sociology graduate?' The answer is "A Big Mac and large fries, please.") And in case you think I am pouring scorn on the social sciences, you should know that I did an MA in Applied Social Studies…

As I kiss Tom goodbye, I suddenly realise that this is how it will always be now; he won't be coming home with us, he has chosen to make his way in a city over two hundred miles distant, and that is his home now. While he was a student, his home was still in West Yorkshire, but that is no longer the case. Of course, Bristol is not really that far, and many people have to face the fact that their grown-up children move overseas, so in a way I am lucky; But I do not feel lucky as I load Alex and the jacket into the Fiat Panda and head north.

On the return journey to Yorkshire, the car starts emitting an awful noise, which gradually worsens as we proceed up the M6. The exhaust is broken, and we finally arrive back in Berringden Brow sounding as if we are travelling in a tank. The following day, I leave the car at a garage to have a new exhaust fitted and go into Berringden by bus to take the graduation photographs to be developed. Halfway there, the bus driver suddenly pulls up in a lay-by, lights a cigarette, and pulls out the "Daily Mirror." We passengers wait patiently for five minutes, after all, everyone is entitled to a break, but soon several people become restive and someone asks when we are likely to be making a move.

"We're not going anywhere until I've finished crossword, and I'm stuck on 14 across," replies the driver, grimly. I'm usually quite good at crosswords.

"What's the clue?" I ask, hoping it isn't anything to do with sport.

"Creator of 'Bridget Jones'. Five and eight. Begins with an aitch."

We are in luck, since I know the answer is Helen Fielding, whose younger brothers I taught at my first school, more than twenty years ago. I call out the answer to the driver, who then fills in the squares, folds up his newspaper very deliberately, looks round at his passengers (who are mostly sitting on the edge of their seats with bated breath), takes a last puff of his cigarette, throws the tab end out of the window, and finally starts up the engine. People variously cheer, sigh with relief, and some come forward to thank me and shake me by the hand.

After visiting Boots, I return to the bus station and wait at stand A, where the buses up to Berringden Brow leave. While waiting, I notice Ben the librarian approaching, in company with his partner, Lesley. They are carrying several large bags of shopping, from one of which protrudes a stick of French bread. It looks as though they are going home to cook a delicious meal together. As they wait for their bus, which leaves from the stand opposite, Lesley laughs and gazes up at Ben, while he places an affectionate hand on her shoulder. I feel a slight pang, as it is often quite difficult, this being serene, single, self-sufficient and celibate... Ben and Lesley's bus is leaving from the stand opposite mine, and with eyes only for his companion, Ben does not notice me.

Chapter 8

My godson, Luke, is being baptised on Sunday. My problem is that I am still without a car, as it apparently requires more than simply the exhaust, and I have to get from Berringden Brow to the other side of Manchester on a Sunday morning by public transport in time for the baptism service at 10.30. According to the bus and train timetable, this is possible in theory, if I arise at dawn and catch the first bus, connecting with a train to Manchester where I can get a taxi. It would not do for Luke's godmother to arrive late, since it might look like the lazy fairy bestowing an unwanted gift of tardiness.

Alex is to accompany me, as he likes babies. We leave in good time to catch the bus, but there is no sign of it. We wait impatiently, but it clearly is not going to turn up. There appears to be no help for it but to hitch-hike to the station. I stick out my thumb, but people passing by in cars appear so startled by the sight of a dishevelled middle-aged female hitch-hiker that they drive on at speed. Then I notice a taxi approaching, and joyfully hail it, but it is already on hire. It does not look as if we will make the baptism, and I am beginning to feel very despondent, when Alex shouts that the taxi has pulled up further down the road. We run towards it, and a lady leans out of the window, explaining that she is going to into Berringden, if that will help. We jump in gratefully, and I explain about the missing bus, the imminent departure of the train and the 10.30 baptism service. She says that she noticed the look of desperation on my face as she passed, and the taxi driver says that Sunday morning is a notoriously bad time for public transport. We are whisked to the station, pay half the cab fare, and throw ourselves onto the Manchester train.

However, our problems are still not over, as we fetch up at a station close to an out-of-town shopping centre, with not a taxi in sight. As we hurry towards the shops to look for one, we come across a pair of abandoned supermarket trolleys. Alex leaps on one and, using it as scooter, is soon way ahead of me, so I have no choice but to gingerly follow suit, stowing my handbag and the carrier containing Luke's christening gift into the trolley and carefully scooting along the asphalt. When we reach the shops, there is still no sign of a taxi, nor are there any buses to be seen, so it seems we have to hitch-hike once again.

I flag down a lady motorist as she is about to leave the car-park and ask her which way she is heading. She says she is going in the opposite direction to the church, but on seeing my face fall, she says she will take us anyway, as it is not far. I thank her profusely, and sink into the passenger seat exhausted, clutching the presents, and feeling almost as if I have traversed the best part of the globe this morning, instead of the twenty or so miles from Berringden Brow, by taxi, train, hi-jacked car and supermarket trolley. Michael Palin on his world-wide travels has nothing on us. And so we arrive at the church in time, a little frayed at the edges, and the baptism goes off without a hitch. Little Luke does not cry at all, but his godmother has a few tears in her eyes.

"Ah, Amaryllis," is Ben's surprising greeting, as I approach the library counter next day. I tell him that I feel more like a faded rose or shrinking violet than a showy lily. "No, you're Amaryllis," he says firmly, taking my retuned books and quietly refusing to elucidate. Ben has a degree in English, so this must be some obscure literary reference, of which I as a mere social scientist am completely unaware

Later, I look on the internet; there are hundreds of references for 'Amaryllis', most of them to do with gardening, but there is also a novel entitled "Sporting with Amaryllis" the title of which relates to a quote from Milton "To sport with Amaryllis in the shade." Hmm, I don't think this can be what Ben is referring to, as we can never have been said to have a sporting relationship, perhaps some verbal sparring last year but nothing very much of that sort these days. I also discover that Amaryllis was an Arcadian shepherdess, and that the name means 'sparkling'. How charming – and how inappropriate for me in my present besieged, bothered and bewildered state. It must be a long time since I last sparkled. It seems that Ben may be suffering from an overdose of irony.

Chapter 9

Now that I have finished my spell on the fringes of academe, I am returning to my previous life, as a voluntary sector worker at Nick's advice shop. This is located on Queen Street, between the take-away and the Asian tailors, within the urban regeneration area, just to the West of Berringden town centre. The shop is in the heart of a multi-ethnic area, and clients come form all sections of the community – Asian, Ukrainian, African, Caribbean, Cypriot, Serbian, Italian, as well as native Yorkshire, of course. In can often be like the United Nations in Nick's waiting room, with several different languages on the go simultaneously. One of the volunteers speaks a number of South Asian tongues, and clients can bring friends or relatives to translate, so we manage quite well, all things considered.

Unlike other centres, where people sit in anxious silence while they wait to be seen, Nick's shop is usually full of cheery conversation, and hardly anyone minds how long they have to wait before Nick is available to see them. It seems for many that their day would not be complete without a visit to the advice centre, and Nick's shop is therefore very much part of the social scene in Queens Street. People come for a chat, whether they have a problem or not, and then continue on their way to the local shops or the Mosque. In fact, some arrange to meet in Nick's waiting room, not requiring advice at all. Frequently a head will pop round the door with a cheery smile and an invitation to lunch. Nick seems to thrive on hot curry, he has mastered the art of eating it without cutlery, using chapattis, whereas I really prefer it mild and being a messy eater, regretfully always have to ask for a spoon.

My main job is administration, but I help out with advice work when Nick is especially busy. I met Nick several years ago, when we were both working at the Citizens Advice Bureau. In those days I was a hard-up young single parent (so nothing much has changed in that respect, apart from the fact that I am now of course middle-aged), looking for a cheap holiday for myself and two young sons. Someone suggested the Youth Hostel Association, but I was told that it would not be possible for a woman to take two boys as there were no mixed dorms, and the boys needed to be supervised at all times. In those days there were not the same number of hostels with family rooms as there are now, and the YHA's suggestion was that I should look for a single parent man with daughters, as I could look after his children while he supervised mine. I was unable to follow this up as I did not know of any such family, and neither did the YHA. Indeed, they still appear to be decidedly thin on the ground, by far the majority of single parents are women, (although I did meet a widowed man with a young daughter in Africa when Alex and I were visiting Robin in Botswana a few years ago.) Nick, on hearing of my dilemma, had volunteered to come on holiday with us, to take charge of the boys, thus satisfying YHA requirements, and we have remained friends ever since.

I finish work at lunchtime, and pop into the library to borrow a film. Ben leaves his shelving, comes over to me and, without a word, hands me a video. It is a copy of a recently released film called "The Clandestine Wedding. " I expect I shall enjoy it, since Ben knows that I like costume dramas and romances.

I go to the Post Office pay a gas bill, pushing an envelope containing the right money across the counter to the cashier. She tells me that the amount is £20 short of the correct total. I am embarrassed and astonished, as I remember counting the money carefully last night, before putting the envelope on the table, where I would not forget it. Luckily I have enough money in my purse to make up the shortfall. What has become of the £20? I grimly hazard a guess.

I do not really want to believe that Alex is the culprit, but there seems to be no other explanation.

"Alex, where's my £20?"

"Don't know what you are on about."

"Yes you do. There was £20 short when I came to pay the gas bill."

"Mum, I can't help it if you're going dippy in your old age. You must have miscounted the money."

It is so infuriating when men use a woman's age as an excuse for **their** behaviour. I am middle-aged, therefore according to Alex I must be going dippy, when we both know that it can only be him who has taken the money.

(Frank the Barn Dance partner also had a version of this age theory, only in his case, it was that I had gone off sex 'because of my age', when in actual fact I had gone off him.)

Although I cannot prove that Alex has stolen the £20, the circumstantial evidence appears overwhelming; all I can do is to ensure that from now on I do not ever leave money anywhere he can find it. I must always remember to hide my purse or handbag, and not leave any envelopes where he can find them, not even with fairly small amounts like milk money. It will be like living under siege in my own house. I used to put his dinner money for the week in an eggcup, but had to stop this as he began taking the entire £10 and spending it on the first day. So now I have to remember to give him two pounds each morning.

Later that evening, Alex brings a lad home, announcing that his name is Snuff and he is staying the night. I really do not like the look of Snuff, who is thin, shaven-headed, tattooed and appears to be suffering from the after-effects some intoxicating substance or other. When Snuff disappears to the bathroom I grab Alex and conduct a conversation with him in urgent stage whispers.

"Alex, why can't he go home?"

"It's late, Mum, and anyway, he has fallen out with his foster parents."

"I can't say I'm honestly surprised. What is he on?"

"Nothing, he's just a bit tired. He's had a difficult time since he came out of prison..."

"Prison! How old is he? What was he in for? Alex, this isn't a bail hostel!"

"He's seventeen, did a bit of robbery; hey, Mum, just because he's been inside doesn't mean he's not a good bloke – anyway, he's a friend of mine, and this is my home, so if I want to invite him then I can!"

"It's your home, but it's my house! And if he has been inside at age seventeen then this would seem to indicate that he is **not** a good bloke to bring home at dead of night."

At this point, Snuff emerges from the bathroom, smelling of sick.

"Snuff, isn't there anywhere else you can go tonight? I'm not really happy about Alex bringing people home unannounced. Where do you live?"

"Todmorden," says Snuff thickly, swaying about on the landing. Alex hustles Snuff away into his room, and steers him towards a sleeping bag on the floor. Then he returns to the bathroom to fetch a bucket, in case the worst happens during the night.

"But won't his foster-parents be worried about him?" I persist.

"Good point, Mum. Snuff, what's the number? I'll deal with it." From the depths of the sleeping bag, Snuff manages to produce a scrap of paper and Alex disappears downstairs to put the call through.

"Don't worry, Mum, it's sorted," says Alex. I collect my purse, mobile phone, chequebook and credit cards and take them up to my room, where I lock them in the wardrobe, feeling very annoyed with Alex. Why on earth does he have to associate with hardened criminals? Whatever happened to all the nice friends he used to have when he was at primary school, or even as recently as his roller-blading days? I know Alex thinks it is unfair to 'give a dog a bad name', but I am not running a branch of Dr. Barnados, with an ever-open door…although, unofficially, that is exactly what does seem to be happening.

The more I think about it, the better an idea it seems that I should try to move house. As well as Alex inviting undesirables home, there appears to be someone still sneaking into the shed at dead of night, and Gary next door reports seeing figures running through the garden when he got up to go to the bathroom in the small hours. Then sometimes I wake up to hear water running in the middle of the night, and there remains the mystery of the plastic bottles strewn round the garden. What can they be for, and who uses them? And now, to crown it all, I have received a letter from the council, complaining about my honeysuckle, which has encroached into the garden of the neighbour next door on the other side from Gary. The letter states that 'it has had to be trimmed back at the householder's own expense.' Goodness, just how expensive could it have been to cut back a few stray tendrils of climbing plant? People seem to worry about the strangest things these days. However, to show willing, I fetch the secateurs and hack at the honeysuckle.

Two young girls arrive and ask if Alex is in. He is still in bed, but appears when summoned, and tells the girls to wait while he has a quick shower. They sit at the kitchen table and ask if I have any photographs of Alex they can look at while they are waiting. I produce an old album with many pictures of an appealing baby/toddler Alex. As the girls coo and exclaim over the photos, I wonder just when did Alex cease to be appealing and become appalling? The girls, whose names are Emma and Carly, finish looking at the first album and ask if I have any more. I indicate a cupboard-full in the hall – both my boys had very well-documented childhoods. The girls are halfway through the third album when Alex appears and wants to leave, but they prefer to stay longer to look at the rest of the collection. Alex is both embarrassed and pleased at their evident admiration of the pictures of his younger self, and starts washing up a sink-full of dishes, which has been festering since the previous evening. I practically faint with shock, and invite Emma and Carly to come round more often. Meanwhile, Frank has arrived, as there is a Barn

Dance later on. He gives Emma a look best described as barely concealed lechery.

"She's real jail-bait, that blonde one," remarks Frank, after Alex has finished the dishes and escorted the girls to the door.

"Why don't you just say she's a pretty girl?" I complain, since the term 'jail-bait' implies that Emma is some sort of Lolita-type character, whose beauty is calculated to ensnare susceptible middle-aged men, which is not the case.

"And why do you insist on commenting on every woman's appearance when you know I don't like it? I suppose you're going to tell me that all men rate a woman's looks as being most important…"

"Well, you cannot really accuse **me** of that – after all, I did go out with you, " Frank replies. I ignore this remark as being unworthy of any sort of response.

Chapter 10

My friend Claire and I are on our way to Manchester to the opera. Claire is driving, as I am still without a car. After our last operatic excursion, when we suffered from the unwanted attentions of fellow members of the audience whilst sweltering in the heat-wave which was the upper balcony, we had vowed not to go again unless we could afford to take a box. However, we have relented, as I have been given two pairs of tickets, for 'Don Giovanni' and 'La Traviata.' The tickets are for seats in the front stalls, and I am very pleased with myself for managing to get them, as a result of a complaint made while I was working in Bristol. I had tried to book to hear 'The Magic Flute' at the Hippodrome, but had been turned away as I wanted only a cheap single seat. The booking clerk had told me that for some reason linked to the computer, those seats could only be sold in pairs, while the only single seats available were twice the price. None of the people I worked with cared for the opera, so I only required one seat. I therefore enquired, with justifiable indignation, why the theatre, not to mention the computer, was discriminating against single people. The clerk sympathised, but repeated that the computer had been programmed to book seats in that price band only in pairs, so there was nothing he could do.

Incensed, I had promptly written a letter to the local paper, explaining that I was newly arrived in the city and had been looking forward to taking advantage of the cultural opportunities available, only to be met with the astonishing news that people could not go to the opera on their own unless they were prepared to buy an expensive seat! I copied the letter to Radio 4's 'You and Yours' programme for good measure.

I was soon contacted by a producer who informed me that it was planned to include a 'Lonely Hearts' type feature in the programme for the following Tuesday. My reaction was 'No, no, no' – he had missed the point entirely – single people had a perfect right to attend the opera unaccompanied, without wishing to be categorised as 'Lonely Hearts.' Somewhat taken aback at my vehemence, the producer said he would make this clear, and asked me to record an interview over the phone. I explained that, while I was aware that going in two by two was a requirement for entry to Noah's Ark, I had not realised that this stricture also applied to the Bristol Hippodrome.

"Oh great! I love it!" enthused the producer, adding that the programme would also ask the theatre manager for his side of the story.

The broadcast on Tuesday began with the Lonely Hearts piece, followed by the "Queen of the Night" aria. "Lovely, isn't it," commented the presenter, adding, apropos of the previous item, that when Jess Greenwood had tried to go to the theatre to hear it, she had definitely *not* been looking to meet new friends or improve her social life; no, Jess had been planning to go **alone**. My recorded piece was then played, followed by an interview with Perry Davies, the manager of the group of theatres, which includes the Hippodrome. He admitted that there had been a mistake, and assured me over the airwaves that if cared to get in touch with him, he would see what he could do, adding that he himself was single and resented paying single supplements.

Naturally, I rang his office straight after the broadcast, and left a message. Perry called me back, full of apologies, to say that the Bristol staff had been given the wrong information. He had since taken steps to ensure that the error did not recur. So it was agreed that I could have two free pairs of tickets for the opera at the associated Manchester theatre. He also kindly arranged to meet me, and my guest, for pre-performance drinks.

Claire, who is continually on the look-out for well-off, presentable new men, is all agog. "What does he sound like?" she asks, as we leave the motorway.

"Welsh," I tell her. Claire wonders if he is rich – she seems to think that theatre mangers must receive enormous salaries. "Let's hope he is good-looking," she adds, as we approach the theatre, free tickets in hand.

Perry has told me to ask for him, and soon we are being escorted upstairs to the comfortable lounge reserved for the exclusive use of patrons. Perry rises to greet us. Much to Claire's barely concealed delight, he is quite attractive, in a tall, bespectacled, professional-looking way. He courteously provides us with drinks and programmes, and reiterates his apologies for the misunderstanding at Bristol. He apparently sells lots of single tickets. He then goes on to talk about his dog, which accompanies him on his travels around the country, visiting all the theatres for which he is responsible. Claire and I cannot contribute much to the conversation, as neither of us owns a dog, and it therefore comes as something of a relief when the bell sounds, and we have to make our way to the stalls, escorted by the assiduous Perry, who invites to return during the interval. When we are safely installed in our seats, Perry leaves us and disappears backstage. I know by the way that Claire keeps trying to catch my eye that she wants to discuss Perry, but I keep my head down, quietly studying the programme, until the conductor enters the auditorium and obliges Claire to pay attention to Mozart rather than Davies.

During the interval I seek out the plush executive loo en route to the Members' bar. When I arrive upstairs, Claire and Perry are in conversation, Claire smiling sweetly across the table at Perry, who is still doing most of the talking.

Perry mentions a theatre premiere he attended earlier in the week, a glittering occasion, by all accounts. Ever the attentive host, he goes to fetch me a drink, and Claire takes the opportunity to tell me that he has mentioned that he liked my sense of humour, as evidenced by the Noah's Ark comment on the radio.

Returning with my glass of wine, which I have to drink rather quickly, as the interval is almost over, Perry explains that he will have left the theatre by the time the performance ends, but that he will ring me next week. (Oh for a pound for every time I have heard a man utter those immortal words...) So, my off-the-cuff broadcast comment has unexpectedly been rewarded with excellent free seats, plus an evening of Perry's solicitous attention. He could not have done more – yet, I have the impression that he would really have much preferred to spend the time walking his dog. I do not blame him for this, since I, too, would have felt rather more at ease with the dog.

"Well," says Claire later, glancing sideways at me as we head eastwards along the M62. "Did you fancy him?" We are not of course discussing 'Giovanni', but Perry.

"Not especially; he was extremely polite and attentive, but he did not fancy me either. Anyway, you know I have given up on men." I realise that carnal Claire does not believe me, but after a number of fruitless attempts to obtain a boyfriend, such as asking out Jeremy the churchwarden, using the 'Guardian Soulmates' column to no avail, and chatting up the already-spoken-for (although I did not realise it at the time) Ben the librarian, I have decided it really is not worth the effort. It had been clear from the start that Jeremy and I had very little in common, and I later discovered that Ben was going out with Lesley from the reference library. I had eventually drifted into the highly unsatisfactory relationship with Frank, my Barn Dance partner, which had mercifully ended when I went to work in Bristol.

"You're not still waiting for Robin to return, are you?" asks Claire, referring to my former partner, away teaching in Botswana and living with Tebogo.

"Goodness, no; anyway, he has renewed his contact, and won't be back for at least another two years. Anyway, I am over all that now. And celibacy can have its advantages, you know."

"Hmm, I can't really think of any…besides, aren't you going to hear 'Traviata' on Saturday with some man?"

"Yes but that's Laurie. He is 75, God bless him, and his daughter is my age. He enjoys music, so I am taking him along, as you said you did not want to come on Saturday. It is possible for a man and woman to go out together just as friends, you know."

"I don't think I ever do," muses Claire as we reach the Berringden junction. "Well, if Perry does ring to ask you out, make sure that I am included in the invitation – I could get used to a well-off beau."

"Claire – he won't ring! And if by some chance he does, I shall certainly not even tell you. You aren't planning to take me along if that man at the health club you think fancies you rings up to ask you out, are you?" Claire looks astonished and shakes her head.

"Well then. Goodnight, and thanks for the lift." I get out of the car, wondering why we have spent the entire journey discussing men rather than Mozart. At least things will be different when I go to hear 'Traviata' with Laurie, as Perry will not be present and I can look forward to an untroubled evening simply appreciating the music in the company of a dear old friend.

Chapter 11

I catch the train to Manchester on Saturday and find Laurie waiting on the platform at Victoria to greet me. I suppose you could call Laurie a travel agent, in that he arranges holidays to interesting parts of Europe; but he is unique, in that his clients are his friends - there are probably getting on for a thousand of us by now, although the clientele is becoming increasingly elderly, and some have sadly died, while others have become too frail to undertake the rigours of coach travel. I think I am still one of the youngest on Laurie's list.

What started out as small-scale trips in a minibus after the war, visiting places of especial interest to socialists rather than socialites, has developed over the years, so that Laurie now has no need to advertise, as his holidays fill up on the strength of personal recommendation. Friends tell friends how interesting they are, and these new people tell their associates, and so it goes. Thus it was that I met Robin on one of Laurie's trips, on our way to spend Christmas in Sorrento. I had Alex, then aged seven, with me, his elder brother Tom having elected to spend the festive season with his father, Bill. Both my boys' first experience of 'abroad' was on Laurie's trips, and they have accompanied me to Italy several times, and also to Spain and Hungary over the years. On the long journey to Sorrento, Alex had understandably become rather bored, and had made his way down the coach, chatting to people en route. There was a spare seat next to Robin, who had invited Alex to sit and talk to him. Alex, at that time a great chatterbox, had begun telling Robin about his mother and brother, and for some reason had said that I made wonderful apple crumbles. It was no doubt this revelation of my culinary skills which tempted Robin, yet again and probably against his better judgement, to abandon his single status, since it later transpired that he had been married twice before.

Laurie is always delighted when two of his customers get together, and he was equally sorry when Robin left me to go to Africa. I have been on several of

Laurie's holidays since Robin's departure, usually on my own, as the boys no longer wish to accompany me. Of course, the minute I board the coach and see all the old familiar faces from previous trips, I am not alone. However, I have steered clear of any more holiday romances, having resolved to try to lead a less complicated life. There have been one or two, mostly rather elderly, gentleman, who seemed to take a fancy to me, but I am not looking for a sugar daddy, or for anyone else.

The most recent of Laurie's excursions was to a spa town near Verona, the highlight of the trip being an evening at the opera. I had been happily sitting near the back of the coach with a quiet lady who was travelling with her two daughters, but on the way into Verona, Laurie called to me to come and sit near the front, next to a man called George, a social worker. The reason for this was ostensibly to help with the directions, as I have a little Italian. It seemed that neither Laurie nor the coach driver were sufficiently proficient in the language to read the map, and had taken several wrong turnings. This is not altogether unknown, and indeed forms part of the charm of Laurie's holidays, since we have stumbled across all manner of interesting sights and spectacular views while searching for somewhere else entirely.

On this occasion, there was already a competent Italian speaker, a rather officious lady called Araminta, sitting next to Laurie at the front, so I seemed to be surplus to requirements. I then began to suspect that Laurie's plan might be to sit me next to George, the social worker, in the hope that maybe we would become friends - or perhaps more, as they say in the personal ads. After all, we seemed to be more or less the same age and were both single, and it turned out that George lived only half an hour's drive away from Berringden Brow, but on the Lancashire side of the Pennines. What other travel agent would take such trouble to try to ensure not only that his clients have a happy holiday, but also that they live happily ever after?

I tried to relax and chat with George, but we were somewhat distracted by the rather fraught conversation taking place between those trying to find the right route, with Laurie the courier, Dave the driver and Araminta the Italian speaker all suggesting different directions when we reached a crossroads. We had already stopped to ask a policeman exactly where the Arena was located, and time was pressing, with the performance due to start in twenty minutes.

"Straight ahead!" cried Araminta. "He said '*Per semaphore e a dritto.*"

"No, no, it's *left* according to this map," said Laurie, consulting a street plan.

Dave glanced across and informed Laurie that he had the map upside down, and we should therefore be turning *right*. There was still no sign of the Arena, and the coach was therefore obliged to tour the one-way systems of Verona once more. George and I were sitting on the edge of our seats, anxiously scanning the streets for direction signs, and I was longing to return to my former place at the back, to be oblivious to the route-finding drama, and able simply to admire the Veronese architecture as we passed it for the third time.

Of course, we finally made it to the Arena, and had a marvellous evening, despite the fact that the performance was halted for an anxious ten minutes because of a distant thunderstorm which threatened to come closer and soak us all. In fact a few drops of rain began to fall at one point, and people started putting up umbrellas. Even after the shower, the atmosphere in the Arena was stifling; still, it was a never-to-be-forgotten evening and I was glad to have had the opportunity to experience it, all thanks to dear Laurie, our septuagenarian music-loving Italianophile travel agent and friend.

Afterwards, there was the problem of getting everyone back onto the coach, the vehicle out of the car-park, and once more round the one-way system. But to me, safely hidden at the back once more, none of this mattered. My head was overflowing with Puccini's music, and my heart was full of nostalgia, knowing how much Robin would have enjoyed the evening. I remembered the time on a previous Italian trip, when we had explored Lucca and found Puccini's house together. It is at times like those that I wish that he could have settled down and been content with the pleasant happy life we had led together in Berringden Brow, instead of allowing his restless nature to take him six thousand miles away to Southern Africa, leaving me so bereft.

Tonight, Laurie takes me to an Italian restaurant near the theatre, saying this will remind us of our trips. The performance of "La Traviata" is simply wonderful, and I find I can relax and enjoy the evening more in Laurie's company than was possible the other day with Claire and Perry. Afterwards, Laurie escorts me back to the station, and sees me onto the Berringden train.

"We must do this again," he says "I'll find out what's on at the Bridgewater Hall and give you a ring."

So while I realise that Perry will not call me next week as promised, I know I can rely on Laurie to let me know about forthcoming musical evenings and future trips. Now that is the sort of man I am proud to count as my friend.

Chapter 12

The phone rings, and it is Robin 's voice, calling from South Africa, on a cell-phone, to let me know he is coming home for good. He will need to have somewhere to stay for a while at first, until he can get himself sorted out, and wonders if it will be possible to stay with me. He says he is coming quite soon, even though the African school term has not yet ended. I say, "Yes", and he immediately rings off. I then try 1471, forgetting that it does not operate when someone has called from overseas, a voice simply says that they do not have the caller's number. So I can do nothing more but wait for him to arrive.

For nearly five years I have wondered how I would feel if this day ever dawned. I had convinced myself that Robin would remain in Botswana forever, or at least until he retired. Then, after he had been in hospital with some life-threatening tropical illness, I was afraid that he might die there. And now he is coming home and I feel calm, not even mildly puzzled that he is not waiting to finish his contract, since nothing that unpredictable man does can surprise me now. I suppose he can have Tom's room, as Tom no longer uses it, and Robin did say his stay would be only temporary. I had better look out clean bedding and tidy up – he said he would be here quite soon, and with Robin that could mean hours rather than days. Indeed it is possible he will be on tonight's flight from Johannesburg, since he has already left Botswana. Then he will have to make his way from the airport, so I calculate that the earliest he can reach Berringden Brow will be tomorrow evening

I switch on the radio, only to hear that the famous actress has died. I wonder how her proud father, my neighbour Wilf, has taken this sad news, and imagine he may have hit the bottle in a big way, so call at the flat to offer my condolences. Myrtle lets me in, and to my surprise I find a completely sober Wilf tidying up a cupboard.

"Wilf, I've heard the news. I'm so sorry."

"Thank you, Jess, lass. Aye, they rang me last night from the hospital to tell me. But they've got her age wrong in this morning's paper; she wa' 71, not 70. She had her birthday last month. Leukaemia or no, she had a wonderful life."

Wilf shows me the obituary, which carries a lovely photograph and lists some of the many stage, film and television parts played by his illustrious daughter. I sit with Wilf looking at pictures of her. Myrtle offers me a cup of tea, and after I have drunk it Wilf returns to his cupboard while Myrtle shows me out.

"It's hit him hard, " she whispers. "Even when it's expected, it's still a shock."

That's the danger of living a long life, I suppose – that your children may pre-decease you, the saddest thing imaginable, as has also been the case with my dear aged god-mother in Devon, Auntie Phyllis, whose son and daughter, themselves both childless, died in middle age.

I had better get more food in since Robin is coming. Butternut squashes are expensive here, but Robin likes them and so do I, (they always remind me of Botswana where they are plentiful and cheap.) I also buy mushrooms, tomatoes, courgettes, aubergines and onions, so my bags feel very heavy as I walk through the precinct. Perhaps I'll have a reviving bowl of homemade soup in the health food café.

I stagger up the stairs and collapse inelegantly into a chair next to the shelf where the newspapers are kept. Picking up the "Yorkshire Post", which carries a front page obituary of the famous actress, I realise that I have left my reading glasses at home, so have to squint at the story while holding the paper some distance away from my nose, with arms outstretched. It is then, glancing over the top of the paper, that I realise Ben is sitting at the next table, facing in my direction, head bent in close conversation with a lady whose back is turned towards me, but who appears to be his partner Lesley. Perhaps I should leave, as I do not want him to look up, notice me, and think I followed them in deliberately; but then again, I don't really want to go anywhere else with my heavy bags, and he may very well have already seen me come in; after all, I made enough noise struggling up the stairs. It would look strange if I left now. So I decide to stay put, and order my soup when the waitress arrives.

Ben and Lesley finish their meal. Ben goes to the counter to pay, while his companion goes downstairs to look round the health-food shop. Since I am sitting right next to the open door leading onto the stairs, everyone has to pass close by me as they leave. I check that my shopping bags are safely under the table, since I do not want anyone to trip over and fall headlong downstairs, as if I had left my packages lying about untidily on purpose, in the manner of a woman scorned. As Ben passes, I look up from the paper, which I am still struggling to pretend to read, and say 'hello'. Ben nods and returns the greeting. I feel this would be an altogether inappropriate moment to strike up a conversation by telling him I enjoyed the "Clandestine Wedding" video, and anyway the waitress is bringing my soup.

Chapter 13

Robin arrives even earlier than I had anticipated, having caught an overnight flight to Manchester rather than Heathrow. He has very little luggage with him, only a small rucksack, as the rest of his things are being sent on by sea and will hopefully turn up in six weeks' time. Having left the heat of Southern Africa for the autumn chill of Yorkshire, Robin is feeling the cold. I advise him to go to the local charity shop to obtain warm clothing. However, before we go, he looks through the recesses of my wardrobe, territory into which I seldom venture myself, and discovers a few long-sleeved shirts and jumpers, which must have been there since before he went away five years ago and have escaped my periodic purges. Joyfully reunited with his old clothes, Robin decides to postpone his shopping expedition in favour of a visit to the library. However, when we get there it is shut. Of course, I should have remembered, the place is closed for a week in order that a new computer system can be installed. The citizens of Berringden will have to manage without the library until next Monday morning. Last year, I would have found this very difficult, but of course, these days I can accept it with equanimity.

"Come on, Robin, it's brightening up, so let's go to Saltaire for the afternoon."

This was always one of our favourite places when we lived together.

"Good idea, old bird, we'll look round the mill and I'll buy you afternoon tea."

For some reason, it seems I am now called 'old bird'. Rather unflatteringly, for what with Frank likening me to a badger and now Robin calling me an old bird, I am beginning to think I should be living in the woods. Although, of course, I cannot leave home, as I am running a half-way house for waifs and strays, what with Robin in the spare room, Nick inexplicably sleeping on the sofa, even when he has a perfectly good bedroom at his mother's house, and Alex bringing home strange lads for snacks and sleepovers. (Various dubious-looking characters keep arriving, all having one thing in common, since they are always clutching empty plastic water bottles. I still have not got to the bottom of the plastic bottle mystery, but hope that now I have a man officially in residence the vandalism in the garden and shed will stop).

At first, I enjoy having Robin back, although of course we are now just friends rather than partners. He says he needs some time to readjust to life in the UK, which I can understand, expecting him to be with me perhaps until Christmas. However, Robin shows no sign of wanting to find either a job or a place of his own to live. He has discovered the benefits of being an almost destitute older person in present-day British society, since he is now in his early sixties and qualifies for the minimum income guarantee, housing benefit, the heating allowance, and a card for cheap coach travel. He is not required to seek work or sign on, so can please himself what he does. Personally, I can't wait to be sixty – but by that time I expect they will have altered all the rules so I will have to work until I drop. Actually, I feel as if I am about to drop nowadays, what with work and worries about Alex, not to mention the demands of all the various lodgers and vagrants. I fall through the door one tea-time, with an armful of groceries, at which Robin, disturbed by the commotion, emerges from the front room, where he is watching television. There is no sign of any cooking under way, not so much as a kettle has been boiled. The house is warm, with the central heating apparently going at full blast.

"Are you all right, old bird?"

"Not really - could you give me a hand with these bags?"

"I will in a minute. I'm just watching the end of "The Weakest Link." Hmm, how very appropriate.

As I finish decanting the shopping from the carriers into the cupboards, Robin reappears. "And what were you thinking of cooking for tea tonight, old bird?"

"I don't know. I hoped you might have started something."

Robin bridles. "And why you should presume that? I've had other priorities."

Oh, no, the same old refrain. This is what he used to say five years ago, when we were living together. Other unexplained priorities, always unconnected with the daily routine of shopping, cooking, washing and cleaning.

"And what exactly would they be? Are they concerned with getting a job or finding accommodation?" I foolishly ask Robin, knowing full well the response I will get.

"Just because I choose not to discuss my business with you does not mean to say that I don't have important things going on."

"Well, even though I don't know what you are up to, I did hope you might find some time to help me round the house."

"I never tell you my business because I operate on the 'need to know' system - and you don't need to know. Nobody helps me solve my problems, but you seem to expect me to help you with yours!"

"I simply expect people living under my roof to pull their weight." I realise that this is like a red rag to a bull.

"Well, get that idle fucker upstairs to do something." Robin is referring to Alex.

I decide that it is useless to point out that Alex has at least been to school and done a paper round today. I am too tired and hungry. Instead, I go to the kitchen and start heating frozen pizza and oven chips. By the time they are ready to eat, Robin has had a change of heart. He announces that he will make a stew for tomorrow's tea. I tell him I will look forward to it all day.

Later that evening the phone rings. When I answer, I hear a strange voice asking for Alex, but Kenny has called for him and he is not in. On being told this information, the voice sounds disgruntled. "Tell him I want my money," it says, before ringing off. I dial 1471, but the caller has withheld their number.

When Alex comes in I ask him, "Who is it, and what money do you owe him?"

Alex is evasive. "It's just some bloke in Hebden. I don't owe him very much."

"How much? It's enough for him to ring and remind you, anyway."

"Hardly any at all! Listen, Mum, I'm knackered, and I'm off to bed now."

"All right, but I don't want you borrowing money from people – ask me first."

"Mum, you wouldn't understand and I don't want to talk about it," is Alex's parting shot before retiring upstairs. It all sounds deeply suspicious to me, and I resolve to get to the bottom of it in due course, although not tonight. Alex is evidently another household member operating on the 'need to know' system.

And of course, I never know where Nick is in the evenings or what he is up to, he simply comes in at midnight after everyone else has gone to bed, sleeps on the sofa in a sleeping bag, then gets up early and goes off to work before the other residents are up and doing. I catch up with him when I arrive at work, by which time there is always a room full of clients waiting to see him. So although living under the same roof, it is as necessary for me to make an appointment in order to have a conversation with him as it is for any client. What a household – and whatever happened to my longed-for quiet life?

Chapter 14

The library has re-opened, having had its new computer system installed. As I cross the threshold, I am greeted by Ben, bowing low in an elaborate courtly gesture. What a welcome! I wonder if all library subscribers are being treated this way, or only those of us nicknamed Amaryllis…

At teatime, I dash through the door, eagerly anticipating not having to cook a tasty stew. However, to my disappointment, there are no welcoming savoury smells. On the kitchen table I notice four cans of beer and three onions. Robin is in his usual chair in the front room.

"Robin, you **are** the weakest link, goodbye," I chime in with Anne Robinson. "What happened to the stew?"

"I didn't have time to make it, and anyway, I couldn't find anything to put in it."

"Well, we live two minutes from a shop – and you must have been out today as you have bought some beer and onions."

"Yes, I went to Nether Berringden on the bus."

"But they have that big Tescos there in the main street!"

"Do they? I didn't notice it…"

I realise that it is pointless to pursue to conversation, and return to the kitchen. Rummaging around in the cupboard, I find some potatoes which look as if they need using up, and put them in the microwave. They I make a salad.

"Do you want tuna or cheese or baked beans on your potato?"

"Cheese, I think. Perhaps a few beans also. Don't go to too much trouble."

That evening, as I am trying to watch a video, Robin decides to call Tebogo in Botswana. The phone is in the front room, and since it is fixed to the wall and not the sort you can walk round the house with, so I am obliged to listen to Robin or leave the room. I remain. After all, it is my house and my telephone. Also, I have to admit that I am quite curious to hear what he has to say to her. I must explain that Robin always pays for these calls, it is not the expense, but the fact that he uses my phone to call his African lady-friend which annoys me. Tebogo's English name is Pat, and that is what Robin calls her, so much nicer than 'old bird'.

54

"Well, Pat, how's it going? How's work? What's the weather doing – as if I need to ask…"

Robin then goes on to enquire after the health of Tebogo's daughters, away at university; and, rather worryingly, suggests that they must visit England at some stage, and that he will look after them. And just where is he going to accommodate them? I really cannot cope with any more lodgers, as all the bedrooms are taken I already have Nick sleeping on the sofa.

Having talked cheerily to Tebogo for ten minutes, Robin puts down the phone with a final, "See you before too long, Pat; we'll have a laugh and a chat."

I feel I must challenge him about the young women's proposed visit.

"Where are they to sleep if they visit?"

"Don't worry, I will make arrangements. It's none of your business anyway."

"Fine, but I just want to make it clear that there's no room for them here."

"So much for your hospitality, Jess, if I'm not allowed to have people to stay." Robin flounces out of the room before I can reply. He is being very infuriating, as I have already said he can have his friend Charlie for a weekend. However, the prospect of providing accommodation for long-stay visitors from overseas is very different from having Charlie here for an odd night.

I try to settle down to the video, but realise that it is not the one I thought I had borrowed, which was 'The Story of 1900'. It seems that what I have actually been issued with is something rather appropriately entitled 'Strange Days'. Both are set on ships, but are very different stories. Maybe this indicates teething troubles with the new computer system. I phone the library, which is on late opening until eight o'clock. Ben answers and I explain the problem.

"Strange Days indeed," says Ben, adding that I can rent another film for free.

The next day, Robin announces that he is off to visit his relations in Scotland. So much for having a man about the house.

Alex brings home a form for the forthcoming Parents Evening at his school. There are various appointment times already filled in for a number of subjects, and it seems that we will be there for at least two hours.

"It's going to be a long evening, Alex," I remark.

"Yeah, you'd better take a good book,"

"You as well. Have you finished "Of Mice and Men?"

"Get real! I'm not coming!"

"But I thought that was the whole idea – to have both pupils and parents there to talk about your work and GCSE prospects."

"Mum, you don't have to go and sit in the school hall for two hours to find out that I'm crap at lessons and won't pass any GCSEs, 'cos I can tell you that now. Remember last time – you said you felt like crying afterwards."

It's true. His teachers had all told me that Alex was either 'laid back', 'lazy', 'poorly motivated', 'a dreamer', essentially variations on a theme. Alex has frittered away his school days, ever since reception class. Yet at all the Parents Evenings I have religiously attended over the past decade, his teachers have always emphasised how well he is capable of doing, if only he would work…

" I hoped you might have improved a bit since then, what with it being closer to the exams."

"Well, I haven't, so don't waste your time. Get a video, or have a night out with your mates or something."

"OK; I don't see why I should put myself out if you won't. After all, it's not me taking the exams. I passed all mine years ago."

"Yeah, yeah; we know you're brilliant, no need to rub it in."

"I was never brilliant, Alex, just hard-working."

"Yeah, always hanging about in libraries doing homework. What a sad life you must have led - no cigs, no ale..."

"I had other ways of enjoying myself, Alex."

"You've told me - teaching Sunday school, being secretary of the youth club, helping your mum with the am-dram group...."

"Well, there are worse ways of spending time."

"Mum, you're a complete saddo."

Next day I find the following message from the school on my answer-phone.

"We understand you have decided not to attend Parents Evening this term. We are very disappointed to hear this. **We** have not given up on Alex and find it regrettable that you appear to have done so."

"Alex, what exactly did you tell the school?"

Alex shrugs. "I handed the form back and said you couldn't be arsed to go."

"Thanks, son."

Chapter 15

There is to be a poetry evening in a barn attached to a house up the road, a fund-raising event organised by Victoria, a lady from church. The well-known actor Barrie Rutter is to read from the work of Ted Hughes, the late poet laureate. I walk up in the pouring rain, and find the barn, warm and candlelit. As I am handed a welcoming glass of wine, I look round and notice several people I know, including Dylan, a middle-aged man who lives up the valley, so I say hello to him. He tells me he is keen to support literary events, since he himself writes. I make the mistake of telling him that I do also, having had a few articles and short stories published. Then the reading starts, so we all sit down on the benches and straw bales arranged around the barn. During the interval, I chat with hypochondriac Phil, whom I originally met via the Guardian Soul-Mates column; it was immediately quite apparent that we could never be soul-mates, but we became friends instead. Phil tells me about his plans to go on Voluntary Service Overseas. He had asked to go to Africa, but they are sending him to Bulgaria instead. I enjoy the evening, as it is one thing to trawl through Ted Hughes's poems for O level, and quite another to hear them read so beautifully in such atmospheric surroundings.

At the end, Dylan waylays me at the door, asking if I would like to accompany him to the local pub for a drink. I really do not want to go, and make some excuse about the rain and wanting to get home before it becomes even heavier. Dylan then asks me to name a day during the following week when I will be available. My heart sinks, and I tell him I am busy all next week.

"Are you sure you can't go now?" Dylan persists, "We both have umbrellas."

It seems quite inescapable that I should have to have a drink with this man.

"Oh, very well, " I sigh, and we splash down the hill to the "Wild Rover". However, at the door of the pub, Dylan stops and exclaims that he has just remembered he has no money.

"Goodness, neither have I! Well, that's it, I'm afraid," I run off home as quickly as I can, before Dylan can suggest another date, hoping that he cannot hear the coins jingling in my pocket.

At home, I find Alex in his room, watering some attractive green plants.

"These are nice, Alex; what are they? I don't think I've seen these at the Garden Centre. Where did you get them? I don't think they'll do very well here, though; there's not enough light. Why don't you put them on the front room window-sill?"

Alex mutters something about having got them from a lad in Hebden Bridge, and wanting to keep them in his room so he can look after them. I am puzzled by Alex's sudden interest in horticulture, until realisation dawns on me, and I know why he does not want the lovely plants displayed on the front room window sill, in full view of all passers by.

"Alex, you must get rid of those cannabis plants, attractive specimens or not!"

"Don't worry; I'm only going to press the leaves to make Christmas cards."

Well, it's a novel excuse, but I doubt it would impress the law enforcement agencies, should they choose to visit. I have heard that they fly helicopters with heat-seeking devices over people's houses to detect the presence of cannabis plants growing in attics. But it does seem a shame to get rid of such beautiful plants, so I give Alex the benefit of the doubt. The plants can stay another week, after which they must be used for Christmas cards or binned.

There seems to be a lot happening on the cultural front, as now Victoria has invited Claire and I to attend the world premiere of a dramatic work entitled "Socks!" celebrating the Yorkshire woollen industry, with special reference to the hand-knitters of Dent Dale. This is to be held in a converted textile mill in Berringden, owned by Victoria's family. I hope she has not also invited Dylan.
To our astonishment, when we are ushered to our seats, we find them already occupied by knitting needles and balls of chunky white wool; it is apparently an interactive performance, and the audience is invited to knit throughout.

"Oh really!" mutters Claire. "I was never any good at knitting." She places the wool and needles under her seat and clasps her hands together in her lap.

"Well I was quite good at it, but when the house lights go down, I won't realise if I have dropped a stitch.."

I start to worry, as no patterns have been provided, and if the theme is socks, aren't they usually knitted with a set of four double pointed needles? I rack my brains, but cannot remember how to turn a heel. The lights are dimmed and the performance begins. "Yan, Tan, Tethera," the old shepherds' counting system, set to song and dance. And so the show continues, accompanied by the click of knitting needles and clicks of exasperation from those knitting, as stitches are dropped and balls of wool become tangled in the semi-darkness. Meanwhile, the man next to me is valiantly struggling to cast on, and as we are in the front row, his groans of frustration are in danger of disrupting the show. I take pity on him, seize his knitting needles and cast on a row. He whispers his thanks, saying he will buy me a drink later. At the interval, I have completed several rows in plain, purl, garter and stocking stitch and am trying to remember how moss stitch is done, since I am finding the knitting rather more enjoyable than the performance. By the time the show ends, I have practically completed half a sock, and other members of the audience are exclaiming at how well I have done as they pass by. I leave my knitting on the seat as requested, wondering what will become of it. We really ought to have been asked to do Oxfam blanket squares, which would have been useful than fragments of sock. Still, it is supposed to be an artistic experience, rather than a knitting circle. We repair to the bar, where the grateful man from the next seat buys me the promised drink, before retuning to Sheffield with his friends. Claire, of course, is disappointed to discover that he lives so far away.

"Imagine coming all the way from Sheffield only to spend the evening wrestling with wool!" exclaims Claire. As world premiers go, I suspect it has been has been rather an unconventional one, but it is good to know that provincial Berringden is in the forefront of alternative theatre. Although actually, I still think I prefer J. B. Priestley…

Chapter 16

Tom is coming home for Christmas. He is supposed to be arriving on Friday evening, but by eleven o'clock there is still no sign of him, and no message has been received. Tom does not want a mobile phone, so I cannot contact him. I go to bed, imagining that he has had to change his travel plans and will now arrive sometime tomorrow. However, just before midnight, Tom rings to tell me that he is at a fish and chip shop in Heptonroyd, and will I collect him. (I now have the Fiat Panda back from Nick's back-yard used-car salesman friend.) I therefore have to put my coat on over my pyjamas and dash off into the chilly night. He is waiting on the pavement, as the chip shop has closed.

"Sorry to drag you from your bed, I missed the train I wanted to catch and had to get the last one," Tom apologises.

"That's all right, you got here in the end. But why were you phoning from the chip shop? Has the phone box been vandalised?"

"No, but I've no money. I asked the man in the chippy as a favour, cos I couldn't buy any chips either, In fact I'm starving, got any pot noodles?"

Now I know why I buy convenience foods, often against my better judgement. They are invaluable for feeding sons and lodgers at short notice.

The following day, (well, later the same day, really,) I go to buy a Christmas tree, as both my sons have lamented the lack of one in the house. In previous years, I have always gone to Berringden Brow garden centre, but this has now closed since the well-earned retirement of the old gentleman who ran it for fifty years. I imagine I will have to pay a small fortune for a real tree, but my family will be satisfied with nothing less. It has started to rain heavily, but nothing can be allowed to deter last-minute Christmas shoppers. While I search the busy street of Berringden for somewhere to park the car, I notice a lovely Christmas tree, complete with a few bedraggled decorations, lying in the middle of the road, causing a traffic hazard. It looks as if it could have been heaved out of an office window after an uproarious Christmas party. I get out of the car to move it to the side of the road, when a thought occurs to me, that I may as well take it home – if it has to be moved for reasons of public safety then it might as well be moved into the boot of my car. Luckily, I have a hatch-back, and the back seats are already down as I was intending to buy a tree anyway. Of course, what I am doing is technically theft, but I prefer to look at it more in the light of adopting an abandoned plant. The street, the tree, and me are all soaked, but I have cleared an obstacle from the public highway and in doing so saved myself a small fortune. And back at home, everyone agrees that it really is a lovely tree...

Later, Tom and I return to Berringden as he wants to go to the library. He says the music collection in Berringden rivals that of Bristol, and enjoys looking through the new acquisitions each time he comes home. I seem to remember that Bristol has more classical and opera, whereas Berringden, with Ben in charge, has an enormous variety, with more of the type of music which appeals to younger people. Tom roots through the CD racks, while I examine the new film releases. Ben is busy behind the counter, but when things quieten down, he approaches with a copy of a folk magazine.

"Something there to interest you, Amaryllis." Ben indicates an advertisement for a Spring concert tour by the Soweto String Quartet, then returns to the counter. The closest venue to Berringden is Bridgewater Hall, Manchester.

"Thank you, that looks good, I'll make a note of it." I return the magazine to Ben, who replaces it behind the counter. I wish him a Merry Christmas, but he just sighs, saying that the festive season is simply something to be endured.

"Bah humbug to you, too, Ben. Maybe things will turn out better than you expect." Ben merely makes a face. Oh dear, he appears to be suffering from seasonal stress, like so many others at this time of year.

Tom and I fight our way through the last-minute shoppers and return home to find the house full of savoury steam. Alex is in the kitchen with Robin, wearing a tea-towel round his waist, industriously peeling potatoes. Meanwhile, there is a pan of stew furiously boiling away on the stove. The table is littered with empty tins and packets, and the floor is covered with onion and carrot peelings, but I do not complain.

"This is a nice surprise, Robin. I did not know you were coming back."

"Neither did I, old bird. Here, Alex, sweep this floor, please." Alex obeys.

I notice that Robin has emptied the washing machine, and spread the laundry out on the radiators. Goodness, perhaps he has made an early New Year's resolution. I doubt it will last, but will definitely make the most of it while it does. I am just thinking about making a cup of tea, when Robin, as if reading my mind, passes me on his way to the sink, brandishing the kettle.

"Out of the way, old bird. My work is never done!"

At tea, I praise the stew, since, although the meat is tinned, the vegetables Robin has added are really good, and there are plenty of them – Robin must have bought up half the market. And he has brought a bottle of wine. Midway through the meal, Nick appears, having missed the bus to his mother's house, where he was due to spend the evening, but managed to catch the Berringden Brow bus instead. Robin serves Nick, while I pour the wine, feeling happy to have all the sons and lodgers round the table together. Christmas has got off to a very good start.

True to his word, Alex has cut all the leaves off the cannabis plants and pressed them under the telephone directory. Now he is sticking them onto folded paper to make very original Christmas cards. He hands me one. It is quite attractive and makes a pleasant change from the more traditional holly.

"Merry Christmas, Mum. You can smoke it afterwards if you like."

"Thanks, but I think I'd like to frame it. It's such a pretty shape and colour."

Then I wonder whether it is illegal to include cannabis leaves in works of art such as collages. It probably is. Maybe holly would have been better after all.

For Christmas, Tom gives me an attractive ethnic handbag, Robin presents me with a bottle of Amarula Cream brought back from Southern Africa, and Alex's gift is a cyclamen plant, bought with some of his paper round Christmas bonus money. He always does well for tips, as he can be very charming to the old ladies on his round. I only hope he has not given them any cannabis Christmas cards, (not that they would be very likely to recognise the pretty leaves as an illegal drug, but you never know.) Alex assures me that his paper round customers have received traditional cards featuring robins and snowmen, nothing which could possibly arouse their suspicions, or that of any visiting relatives.

Nick has not given me anything, so no surprise there. He says he will try to get something in the New Year sales – when he said this last year, I was presented with a shiny new red plastic kitchen rubbish bin. Perhaps this year I might receive some bin liners to go with it, or even some rubber gloves or dishcloths if I'm really lucky.

So there are five of us for Christmas lunch – two sons, two lodgers and me.

On Boxing Day, Nick sets off for Wetherby Races, Tom's dad, Bill, comes to collect his son, and Robin's friend Charlie arrives to drive him to Scotland for the New Year. Alex says he is off to chill with his mates, and I am left alone. After about an hour, I am fed up with doing chores. It is a fine afternoon, so I decide to go for a walk. Wandering along the canal bank, I notice lots of people walking dogs, and wonder how Molly, the stray dog Alex brought home, is doing. All the dog walkers seem to greet each other in friendly fashion, and I begin to think that it might be quite nice to have a dog to walk. Perhaps Molly-the- stray will have a litter of pups this year and we can have one of them, preferably a female. She would be company for me at times like this, when the sons and lodgers have all disappeared.

Chapter 17

Soon it is New Year's Eve, which of course brings with it the performance of the spoof Mummers play written by me and Frank specially for the occasion. As there has been very little opportunity to gather together the various cast members for rehearsal, the thing is a complete shambles. Everyone forgets their lines except me, who has also to try and remember to prompt everyone else, since the official prompter has forgotten to bring her reading glasses. The audience and cast alike are helpless with laughter, and I dread to think what the video will be like – Certificate A for appalling, probably. Afterwards, we go outside to admire the fireworks, and then I drive home through showers of rocket stars and golden rain. By the time I reach the Berringden valley, most of the fireworks have finished, and the world has settled down to nurse its collective sore head as the new millennium begins. I have to drive close to where Ben lives, and as I pass the end of his road I cannot help wondering how he has celebrated. He once told me that it was his custom to watch the old black and white film "The Apartment" at New Year. It is a great film, and I find myself wondering whether I would rather have been watching it with him than fooling around with Frank and the Millennium Mummers. To my relief, I find that my answer is "No;" (this would no doubt also be music to Ben's ears.)

Alex and Nick have both been out celebrating at parties, Alex at a friend's sister's house, while Nick has been to Hesketh and Cory's. The next day, everyone feels fragile, but I am determined not to waste the day. There is a professional performance of some Mystery plays being given at a local arts centre, and I have decided to go. The ticket states that it is advisable to bring refreshments for the interval, since one play is in the afternoon and the other in the evening. I am packing up some soup and sandwiches when I become aware of shouting in the garden. I go out to find out what is causing all the commotion, only to discover Alex and a crowd of about seven other drunken lads baying at me to unlock the shed, which is now on its third padlock. They are threatening to burn the shed down if I do not do as they ask. I remonstrate with them, but am really quite scared, so retreat indoors, where Nick is hiding in the kitchen. I then entreat Nick to come out with me for moral support, and we venture into the garden once more, two quivering middle-aged adults facing an army of hostile drunken strapping teenagers. It really is no contest. We are obliged to run for cover, under barrages of foul language and missiles, (crisp packets and empty cans, but missiles nonetheless,) since retreat appears the safest option. Alex sees me dashing to the car and runs after me.

"Where are you going?" he demands.

"I'm getting out of here, Alex; I'm scared. Can't you get rid of them?"

"They just want the shed opening, so's we can carry on partying under cover."

"But they'll wreck it! Alex, I'm off to the theatre. I'm not letting these oafs upset my plans. Tell them they had better go quickly, as I have called the police."

So this is my Millennium, run out of my own home by Alex's so-called friends.

I have not called the police, I'm calling the oafs' bluff. Happy New Year!

I ring Nick during the interval, and he reports that all is quiet at home, the thugs dispersed as soon as Alex told them the police had been called, and Alex himself is sleeping it all off. I am so glad I did not miss the wonderful performance of the Mystery Plays on their account. The representation of the crucifixion is especially moving, while the scenes set in Hell are lively and scary - in fact the whole thing is stunning. I would far rather be here than at home, cowering under the kitchen table, waiting for the shed to be set alight by a bunch of thugs; better to be watching the artificial flames of this dramatic Hell than our shed ablaze...

Chapter 18

I have been invited to accompany Frank to a Medieval wedding reception. We have to go in appropriate costume, which means trawling through Yellow Pages to find a clothes hire shop which might have some thing suitable. We discover one in Allerton Bywater, of all places, whose proprietor tells us she has a dress in size 16 and a Jester's costume which might suit Frank. I leave my car at the station and proceed to Frank's village by train, where he meets me. We go to find the costume shop, not an easy task, but having taken a number of wrong turnings we eventually discover it, deep in a housing estate.

"Talk about out of the way," says Frank. However, it turns out to be well worth the effort involved in finding it, as I love my dress, cut in a simple flattering style without fuss or furbelows, and Frank looks suitably comic in his yellow red and blue Jester's costume. We head for the reception, feeling very pleased with ourselves. We find knights, monks, merry men, (and quite a few merry women), of all descriptions, swordsmen, archers and peasants. A good times is had all by all, and the wedding video should be highly entertaining.

I change out of my dress and hand it to Frank who is to return the costumes next week, before boarding the train back to Berringden. However, the happy mood of the day is soured when I arrive at the station car-park to find that my car has been broken into. The driver's door is swinging open and the lock is broken and the crooks have attempted to steal the radio. At first I think that nothing has actually been taken, but then I realise that a shopping bag has gone from the back seat. This bag had contained my swimming costume and towel, which I soon find discarded in the nearby churchyard. Then I remember with dismay that I had a video from the library in the bag as well. Of course I can find no trace of it. How foolish of me to leave the bag in sight of passers-by. And what will Ben say when I tell him that one of his videos has been stolen? Will he ban me from the library? Will the cost of replacing it be extortionate, and what about the daily fine for overdue items – will that have to be levied until I can get a replacement? I report the break-in and theft to the police, but only for insurance purposes, as I realise there is no hope of the criminals being found. I drive home and spend Sunday worrying about how I am to face Ben when the library opens.

As it happens, Ben is very good about the whole thing. He cancels the daily fine on the computer, and says that I can delay providing a replacement for a week or so until I can get one second-hand from a video rental store in the town, which sells them off quite quickly for £10 in order to make way for new stock. In my relief, I feel like jumping over the counter and hugging Ben, but luckily for him, the phone rings and he has to answer it.

At home, the freezer door is open, the red danger light is on, the stuff inside is thawing out, and a sticky mess of something indescribable is glooping onto the floor. A discarded pie package in the bin seems to indicate that Nick was the last person to use the freezer. I sigh and fetch the mop. When asked, Nick says he thought the red light simply meant that the freezer was working. I tell him no, that is the green light. I do **not** feel like hugging Nick.

Frank asks me to visit his mother who is in hospital. Over the years, she has alienated most of her friends, relatives and neighbours, and is complaining vociferously that no-one comes to visit her, apart of course from Frank, who dutifully visits every day. I am not especially keen to go, as she never really liked me when Frank and I were going out, because I took her precious son away from her at the weekends. Frank told me she never liked any woman he went out with, except one, Janice, with whom he had an entirely platonic relationship. I tell Frank that this was of course the reason she liked Janice.

"But I never discuss that sort of thing with Mother."

"You don't have to, mothers have a sixth sense about such matters."

I buy a bunch of flowers and accompany Frank to the hospital. His mother appears fairly pleased to see me, but immediately starts telling off Frank.

"Frammy, you didn't say Jess was coming. If I had known I would have put on my other bed-jacket!"

She is using a childhood nick-name for the fifty-plus-year-old Frank. Frank insists that he did tell her, last night, that I was coming, and that anyway, he has just washed the best bed-jacket.

"Good, but did you remember to bring it?"

Frank rummages in his bag, and produces a shapeless pink garment.

"That's not the one! That old thing! That's the second best. You should have brought the blue!" She turns to me with a sigh of exasperation.

"Jess, aren't men hopeless when it comes to these things? What would you do with him?"

I feel like answering "As little as possible these days", but shrug and smile awkwardly in reply. Of course, when you are in hospital with nothing much to think about apart from how ill you feel, I suppose the colour and rank of your night attire does take on this seemingly unwarranted importance. As there is a lull in the conversation now that the pressing matter of the bed-jacket has been fully discussed, I decide to fill in time by going in search of a vase and arranging the flowers. These are carnations of the same shade of pink as the despised bed-jacket, and I nervously return to place them on the bedside table, hoping that Frank's mother will not immediately tell me off for not having brought blue flowers.

Chapter 19

Looking out of the window on my day off, I see a man with a ladder in the garden. I have not commissioned any work, so he must have the wrong house. I enquire which house he is looking for.

"This one. I've come to cut down the clematis."

"I think there must be some mistake. I own this property and have not asked for the clematis to be cut down."

"No, it's the council who's sent me. They own the house next door, and they don't like your clematis growing onto their side."

"Even so, I do think they should have informed me before sending you out. Can't you cut it back from the other side?"

"No, it won't reach. Listen, lady, all this chit-chat is all very well, but my schedule will be completely messed up if I don't get a move on."

"Well, in that case I suggest that you move straight on to your next assignment, as I feel sure that you should not have come into my garden without my knowledge or permission. Please take your ladder and go away."

"I can't do that, it's timetabled here on my schedule."

I stifle an inclination to tell him what he can do with his schedule.

"Then ring whoever has drawn up your schedule and inform I them I don't want my clematis cut."

The man retreats to his van and rings someone on his mobile phone. Then he stomps back into the garden and retrieves his ladder, glaring and muttering at me under his breath. I return indoors and have a cup of tea. To think that had it not been my day off, I would have come home to find my clematis cut down with no word of explanation.

At five o'clock I find an official -looking man on the doorstep, claiming to be from Berringden Council.

"It's about your clematis…"

"OK, before we go any further, please may I see your ID."

The man rummages in his pocket and produces a photo-card identifying him as being a former student of Leeds Metropolitan University.

"This is nothing to do with Berringden Council,"

"No, but you can see it is me."

"That's not good enough – you told me you were from Berringden Council but you don't have the correct ID."

"I **am** from Berringden Council, but I don't seem to have the right card with me. This is the first time I have come out without it, and I really need to talk to you about the clematis…"

"We're not talking about anything unless you can identify yourself properly. After all, we little old ladies are always being warned about bogus officials."

"But I'm not bogus."

"And I'm not having the clematis cut."

I retire to the kitchen once more and have another cup of tea. Well, what a waste of council money, this sending out of operatives without permission and officials without ID. Maybe I should write to the paper about it. I love my clematis, which blooms with a profusion of pink flowers. Maybe I'll cut it back after its next flowering. Or perhaps, even better, I might have managed to move away by then.

The following day I ring a Housing Association, and ask if they are by any chance looking to buy houses in the Berringden Brow area. It seems that they are, but cannot make any further purchases until the new financial year in April. They are apparently extremely short of three-bedroomed properties, and would like to look at mine, so I arrange for one of their officials to view it.

"Be sure to bring the correct ID," I warn him. He assures me he will.

Alex is aghast at the idea of us moving house, as he does not want to leave all his friends.

"Yes, the friends who drink rocket fuel cider and trespass in people's gardens and break into sheds at dead of night. Those dubious characters, who have done time already at age seventeen; why do you think I want to leave, Alex? This business with the clematis is just the last straw!"

"But where would we go?"

"Somewhere fairly local – Hebden Bridge, maybe. Although I don't suppose we can afford the house prices there. It depends what they offer for this place. Or perhaps Heptonroyd. It's nice there, and it has plenty of shops."

Alex flounces out, muttering bad things about Heptonroyd. But now I have finally made the decision to go, I feel nothing but relief.

Chapter 20

Alex has come home very late, soaking wet and without his coat. He also has a nasty cut on his chin. The demon drink has once again done its worst, ably assisted by Alex, of course.

"So where have you been 'til this hour? What a state you're in! What on earth have you been doing? And where's your coat? It's a good one, isn't it…"

"Shush, Mum, don't get heavy! My head hurts – ow - and I'm bleeding."

I clean the gash on Alex's chin with cotton wool soaked in warm water.

"What happened?"

"We were in the 'Crown' and then it got late, we'd missed the last bus, and so we walked along the canal. I must have tripped over a bramble or something."

"You're lucky you didn't end up **in** the canal! But I am vexed about that coat!"

Next day, I resolve to call at the 'Crown' and fetch it on the way into Berringden, and also to ask the landlord why he serves under-age drinkers.

I march into the pub where the landlord looks at me enquiringly. I announce that I am Alex Greenwood's mother, and have come for his coat, whereupon the people sitting at the bar mount a token search. It is nowhere to be found. The landlord says he will look out for it, but I imagine someone else has long since made off with it.

"You do realise that they are under-age, Alex and his friends?"

"Yes, love." The landlord stares brazenly at me.

"And you're still happy to serve them, knowing it's illegal?"

"Yes, love." He never wavers.

"What do you suppose the licensing authorities would have to say about it?"

"I don't care – I'm retiring in a few weeks. You see, love, you can't frighten me. And you have to remember that if your lad and the others weren't in here, they'd be out in the cold with bottles of cider, getting in a dreadful state. At least in here they're warm and I can keep an eye on them."

"But Alex **was** in a dreadful state last night."

"Aye, he was, and I'll tell you for why – it's because he went across the road to the 'Ship' before ever he came in here. I look after those lads, never let them have more than three pints."

"Three! But they shouldn't be having **any** alcohol at all on licensed premises!"

"Let's get real! Of course they're going to drink alcohol! It's the way of lads to drink. And if you try to get this place closed down, then lads'll simply go somewhere else, and all my regulars will lose their local. You'll be doing the village no favours, and folks'll not thank you for it. You know I'm right."

I know he's right. Would it really help the village to lose the 'Crown'? But I hate the idea of people getting away with breaking the law. It seems quite wrong that I can have council officials on the doorstep complaining about my clematis while flagrant breaches of the law at the local go quietly unnoticed.

I return home with a charity shop fleece as a replacement for the missing coat. Alex immediately declares he is not going to wear **that** thing.

"Well, you'll just have to go cold, then. I can't afford to get another good one."

Alex says he will go cold, and swaggers out of the house. Ten minutes later, I find Kenny knocking at the door.

"Alex has sent me to fetch his coat." I hand him the fleece without a word.

Chapter 21

I have a bad cold, but since I have already bought a ticket for a chamber music concert, I am determined to go out this evening. I drive to Berringden and into the car park of the converted former chapel which now serves as an Arts Centre. Now I must mention that I defy the usual stereotype of poor women parkers, and I manage to get the car into a small space right up against the wall. I am just collecting my tissues and keys when a woman raps on the car window.

"Please move this car, as I cannot get into the car park." She indicates a large saloon car at the entrance.

"But I am right against the wall. Atishooo. Atishoo Atishoo."

"Nevertheless, you are in my way."

"Madam, with all due respect, you could get an ox cart through there; well, I could, as I am a good driver. Would you like me to park your car for you?"

"Oh don't be silly!" The woman is obviously not going to trust me, a lowly Fiat Panda driver, with her expensive vehicle.

I notice that the car parked opposite is sticking out rather too much and, between sneezes, suggest that she goes into the centre and pages the owner of that carelessly parked vehicle. By this time, the woman is furious with me, and there is a queue of cars behind her trying to get into the car park. Under normal circumstances, I am a very accommodating soul, but

74

in my present state of health, longing to get into the warm building, and desperate for the loo, I lock up my car and leave her to it. After all why should I be inconvenienced as a result of other people's inadequate driving skills?

I visit the ladies, where I notice my scarlet-cheeked reflection gazing back at me from the mirror, (my vivid complexion being the result of the cold and my fury,) then I flounce into the bar, as there is still some time to go before the performance starts. Who should I find there, with a glass of red wine in his hand, but my former boss, James Habergham, features editor of the Berringden Bugle, the local paper for which I wrote the consumer advice column many years ago. I guess he is here to review the concert.

"Hello, Jess, you look a bit flustered. Can I buy you a drink?"

"Thanks, James, I'll have an orange juice. Atishoo Atishoo."

I realise that in the background there is a commotion going on at the box office, where the lady with the large car is complaining vociferously about not being able to get past a Fiat Panda, and various other people are complaining about not being able to get past a large car. Then the woman storms into the bar, accompanied by the centre manger, and points an accusing finger at me.

"This is the girl who refuses to move her car." Girl indeed!

I feel like replying, "And that's the old bat who doesn't know how to drive hers," but instead suffer a further attack of the sneezes. The manager is asking me to move, while I am trying to explain, that it is actually the red car opposite which is sticking out, so why not page the driver and get him or her to go back against the wall; and anyway, there is room for a double-decker bus to get through if competently driven. James, realising what a poor state I am in, gallantly suggests that he moves my car for me, so I offer him my keys. He returns a few minutes later, with the comment that it would have been perfectly possible to get a pantechnicon through the gap. Then we go into the auditorium. I scrabble in my bag to find my £7 ticket, the root of all my troubles, without which I would have stayed safely at home.

"Pity you had already bought that " says James, "as they always send me two complimentary tickets, and I can't always find anyone who likes classical music."

"Well, I do, so if there is ever a ticket going spare, do let me know. Atishoo!"

"So what are you up to these days, Jess?" James asks in the interval. I explain about the advice centre and Alex, between them enough to keep anyone fully occupied. James has a son of a similar age, but his lad is doing well at school, aiming for university, doesn't smoke, hardly drinks, and is very much against drugs. I sigh with envy. It is Friday night, and I imagine Alex will be staggering home senseless at some ungodly hour, drunk as a skunk, sick as a parrot, possibly having lost his coat, and probably accompanied by shady characters using foul language and expecting me to accommodate them. He and his pals seem to go wild at weekends. James looks startled as I describe life with Alex, and I am rather worried that he will ask me to turn my account into a feature for the "Berringden Bugle." with a headline along the lines of

"Beleaguered Berringden Brow Woman's Battle with Drunks and Dossers,"

I leave promptly after the performance, tired out, and also wishing to escape before the incompetent lady driver of the large car tries to pass the Panda on her way out of the car-park. James gives me a peck on the cheek, promising to email me with news of any future event of interest.

I arrive home, longing for my bed, only to be met by Robin, newly returned from one of his mysterious jaunts, telling me that he has not had his supper, and claiming to be unable to find anything edible in the fridge; and a rather hung-over looking Alex, evidently having been driven home early through hunger, just clearing a plate of left-overs.

"What about that quiche and salad? Atishoo! Have you eaten that, Alex?"

"'Fraid so. And Nick was last seen tucking into the remains of the cottage pie."

Apparently, the cupboard is bare, and as there is nothing worse than a hungry and disgruntled lodger, I prevail upon Alex to run to the fish and chip shop.

Chapter 22

I am on my way by car to visit Tom in Bristol. The group of six former student house-mates has split up, and Tom is now sharing a small house with Rose. I have finally cleared out all Tom's books, comics and annuals and no longer wish to give them house-room. I am also mindful of the necessity of ditching as many unwanted chattels as possible in case I move, so I am now returning these to their rightful owner. There are five large boxes in the back of my Fiat Panda, plus a Space Hopper, which Tom insists he wants me to bring, despite the fact that it would be more suitable to donate it to a Museum of Childhood.

The journey has been straightforward so far, and I stop at six o'clock at the motorway services, to visit the loo and allow time for the city's rush-hour traffic to abate. After a cup of tea, I attempt to start the car, but there is no response from the engine. I am not unduly concerned, as this has happened before, and all it requires is a good shake. I try to shake the car but am not strong enough to free the starting mechanism, so I telephone the breakdown service and explain where I am and what has gone wrong with the car. I am told that someone will be with me soon, and sure enough, a breakdown lorry appears within ten minutes. I ask the driver to give the car a good shake, but he says it will be better to tow me round to the garage, not far away. When we reach the garage, a gaggle of mechanics cluster round my poor old Fiat Panda; I can see through the window that there is much discussion and nodding of heads. Eventually, one of the men comes to tell me that the starter motor is broken.

"Broken! Are you sure it is not just jammed? When this happened once before it was cured simply by giving it a vigorous shake."

"No, no, it's broken this time. Now do you want to continue to Bristol or return home? Cedric here is going to load your car onto the towing lorry and you'll be setting off in ten minutes."

Of course, I do not wish to be towed all the way back to Berringden Brow now I am so close to Bristol, so ask Cedric to head for the city. The Panda is fastened on to the back of the lorry, and I scramble into the cab with Cedric.

"So what happened to your husband?" Cedric asks.

I am quite non-plussed by this as an opening gambit, as in my experience, break-down men usually talk about cars, motorway routes, or remain silent.

"What makes you think I ever had one?" My standard rebuff to anyone asking what I consider to be unnecessary questions about my domestic situation.

"Well, ladies of a certain age, such as yourself, usually do, and you're not *that* bad-looking. Anyway, you must have had one once, as you say you've got a son in Bristol." Oh great, I've simply hired this chap to tow me to Bristol, and now I am trapped in the cab of his truck, with twenty miles of intrusive conversation between here and Tom's. I would sooner have been sitting in the Panda, being towed along behind, than have to put up with idiotic Cedric.

"Haven't you ever heard of parthenogenesis? " I try not to sound too icy.

"Oh well, since you are obviously not keen to tell me about your situation I'll have to tell you about mine." With which, Cedric proceeds to describe his wife, Lani, from the Philippines, and their young daughter, conceived while they were working in Saudi Arabia, to the delight of the prince of the locality, who was apparently so thrilled at her birth that he insisted that she be named after his principality. She therefore has an exotic Arabian name, but is known in the family as Gadget, because of her fondness for the Inspector

78

Gadget television programmes. Every year on her birthday the prince sends her an expensive piece of jewellery. Lani is thirty, Cedric is sixty-three, and Gadget is just four.

"Not bad for an old man, eh?" Cedric comments proudly, glancing across at me in an attempt to gauge my reaction to this news of his attractiveness to young women, and geriatric virility. By this time, I am practically falling asleep, and unable to think of a suitable reply. However, I am saved by the ringing of Cedric's mobile phone. He answers, even though he is driving down the M5.

"Hello, Gadget. What are you up to? Is Mummy there? She's in the bath? Tell her Daddy's on his way to Bristol, and will be home in an hour. Gadget! Stop giggling ...you tell Mummy...you've been watching a video? Which one? Oh that's great. That's your favourite, isn't it...Gadget, listen, I want you to tell...Oh, she's hung up. Oh well. Bright as a button that kid."

Cedric smiles fondly and shakes his head. I long for deliverance. Eventually, we see the lights of Bristol twinkling before us, and I try to explain to Cedric how to reach Tom's house, which is quite difficult, since I have never been there, although Tom has provided me with vague directions. Cedric points out that we will not be able to risk taking any wrong turnings with the breakdown truck. I manage to get to the right general area, then think it best to call Tom on my mobile for exact directions to the house.

"Hi, it's me, I'm on a breakdown truck, we're in Hambleton Road. Where exactly are you from here?"

"Hambleton Road? Never heard of it. Hang on, let me get the 'A to Z'." There is a pause, during which it is clear that Cedric's impatience is mounting, judging by the amount of fidgeting and muttering. Tom comes back on the line to tell me that as he cannot find Hambleton Road in the 'A to Z' it cannot exist.

"Of course it exists! We're in it. We're right by the street sign, it's in the St. Philip's area somewhere, and I don't think it can be far away from you at all."

Cedric, meanwhile, seems about to explode, and declares that he will go into the building we are parked outside and make enquiries, hoping someone inside will have some sense   He disappears into an uninviting-looking establishment, with a blue neon sign proclaiming its name as 'Bar Xotica.'

Two minutes later, Cedric emerges from the place looking quite shocked.

"Blimey, there's girls in there sitting around without any clothes on! I assumed it was just a bar, but they thought I had come in for something else entirely..."

"But more to the point, did they know where Tom's street is?" It is now my turn to become impatient.

"I never got as far as asking them. They thought I required their...services. I was lucky to get out in one piece."

I feel that Cedric is probably exaggerating, and seeing a respectable-looking woman walking her dog on the other pavement, I descend from the cab to enquire directions from her. Tom's street is apparently just around the corner.

Five minutes later, we reach the house, but as there is nowhere to park directly outside, Cedric stops the lorry a little distance up the road, where there is space enough to unload the Panda. As it runs down the ramps onto the tarmac, I reflect that we will have to cart all Tom's boxes of books halfway down the street. I wonder if I can get it any closer? While Cedric is looking for the form which I have to sign for the breakdown company, I jump into the Panda, and without thinking, turn the ignition key. The engine starts first time.

Cedric emerges from his cab, brandishing the required form, with a look of complete astonishment on his face.

"See, I *said* it only needed a good shake." Twenty miles unnecessary towing has apparently done the Panda a power of good, though the downside is of course that I have been obliged to endure more than an hour of Cedric. Every silver lining has a cloud. I

80

wish now that I had sent Tom's books by courier. Except of course that this way, I get to see my son. Here he is, ambling down the street to greet me.

"Hello, Mum, Rose said she thought a breakdown lorry had gone by. You managed to find it OK in the end then? I really don't know where Hambleton Road is, neither does Rose."

"It's not far away, it's the street with 'Bar Xotica' in it. Cedric here went in to get directions." Now that I have arrived safely, I am beginning to see the funny side of it all, so much so that as I can hardly sign Cedric's form for giggling.

"Oh, that place. We were told it was a brothel. So did they know the way?"

"They apparently had more information about positions than directions…"

"Humph!" exclaims Cedric, stomping back to his lorry. He does not appear to have much of a sense of humour, but perhaps young Filipino ladies do not mind this. Next time I break down I shall ask them to try to send a politically correct person with GSOH. Meanwhile, Tom has found the Space Hopper.

"Wow, you remembered to bring this! Thanks Mum!" Tom goes space-hopping down the street, while I am still consumed by giggles, and Tom's neighbours come to their doors to see what is causing all the excitement. I had better get indoors before we are all had up for a breach of the peace.

Chapter 23

Next day, I go into Bristol city centre at teatime to meet my brother, Jeff, who has driven up from Tiverton. This evening there is to be the unveiling of a new statue of Cary Grant, by his widow, Barbara, who was in the same class as Jeff at Grammar School. Cary Grant was of course a native of Bristol. While we wait for the ceremony to begin, Jeff recalls how once after school, when Barbara was saying she would have to go for the bus, he had offered her a lift home, despite not actually having a car. Jeff had dashed round all his vehicle-owning mates, asking if he could borrow a car for an hour. On hearing that it was so he could drive Barbara back to her village, one had readily agreed. (This was the effect seventeen-year old Barbara had on the sixth form boys.)

It is chilly in the December dusk, but Jeff and I, along with scores of others, are determined to stick it out. There is a large screen showing stills and clips from some of Cary's films to entertain the patient watchers and waiters. Eventually, Barbara arrives and is escorted to the statue, where she makes a speech and gracefully unveils the bronze likeness of her former husband. Cary has not been mounted on a plinth, but is poised on the paving stones, as if about to cross the square. Barbara poses to have her photograph taken next to the statue, and is then conducted away. As she passes, I encourage Jeff to move forward and shake her hand, as we are fairly close to the front, but he decides not to do so, as it is such a long time since the days of Tiverton Grammar School and borrowed cars. Both he and Barbara have turned fifty, and I have to say that she seems to have aged a great deal better than he has, as I suppose is often the way with men, who lose their hair, and women who do not. Jeff remarks to me how lovely Barbara looks, and I reply that she always did, except perhaps when playing an old hag in the school play of 1967, which that year was "Love on the Dole." She was Mrs. Bull, the mid-wife and layer out of corpses, and I was playing Mrs. Jike, the gin-swilling spiritualist; we had to exchange our mini-skirts for clogs, caps, shawls, plus wrinkled stockings and faces. I wonder if Cary Grant, himself no stranger to childhood poverty, would have enjoyed the play.

The other reason for my trip to the West Country is so that I can accompany Jeff to an old school reunion, these are of course all the rage these days. The former Head boy, now a retired police officer, has tracked down those of us who have not died or emigrated, and we have been invited to assemble at a restaurant just outside Tiverton. It is truly astonishing to discover how some people have turned out –

Grease Goodwin, for instance, who was always up to mischief, tells me he is now a diplomat. And Carrie Carter, remembered as a shy, awkward little girl, became some sort of super model. I look round the room carefully, trying to sort out exactly who is who – this is much easier with the women, who have not changed nearly as much as the men. These men – decidedly middle-aged, greying, balding, spreading, did I ever have a crush on any of them, help them with their geography homework, or laugh at their terrible jokes? And it seems they are still telling their terrible jokes... Geoff Patrick, whom I recall as being really good-looking, with a fan-club of admiring girls, now tells me he is gay and settled with a partner in West Bromwich. I don't think we really knew what gay was in those days, apart from happy of course, and we had only the haziest idea of the location of West Bromwich. Meanwhile, Jeff has discovered a former girlfriend, while I have found several of mine, and we are all happily reminiscing, with the aid of old photographs of cricket teams, geography club trips, school plays and of course those panoramic pictures, with the whole school sitting motionless for several minutes while those who dared risk the Headmaster's wrath adopted strange poses or made rude gestures as the camera swept by. Those hair-cuts! Those fashions! Those were the days.

Before I leave Devon, I drive to Exeter to call on my aged godmother, Aunt Phyllis, in her bungalow at the top of Pennsylvania. She is now so infirm that she cannot leave the house, but has teams of carers calling morn noon and night, and her kind nephew and his wife also look in every day. Auntie seems contented; she has her cat, her lovely garden and her beautiful view. She asks about the reunion, my brothers and my sons, and I give her edited highlights. I do not stay long, as she gets so tired these days. One thing I am glad to notice is that her hair is as beautifully done as ever – she says the home hairdresser calls each week. Auntie Phyl has always been very particular about her hair, and even at 90 odd, hers still looks very good.

Back in Berringden, I am lurking in the literature section of the library, searching for a copy of "Love on the Dole" when to my surprise, I hear Ben's voice quietly calling my name. However, when I emerge from between the shelves, and see him looking the other way, I realise he is not calling me, but the young woman library assistant presently on the counter. So maybe he gave me the name 'Amaryllis' for no particular reason, but simply because he was finding it complicated having to deal with two Jesses so one of us had to be re-christened. That must be it...

Chapter 24

James Habergham emails to invite me to a performance of "Wild Goose Chase", adding that he does not really expect that I will want to go, since it is only a local amateur production. I say I will be very pleased to accompany him, as I recall my mother's dramatic society putting on this play in the sixties, with her in the part of the dotty archaeologist. (The play appeared rather dated even then, so goodness knows what it will look like these days, although perhaps things have turned round so far that it will now seem quite trendy.)

My mother was a natural comedienne, excelling in farce, and with a great talent for mimicry, and the tradition of amateur dramatics was always strong in our family. For Dotey, trapped in an abusive marriage, it was her chance to escape from the cruel reality of her everyday life, and also an opportunity to shine. She was the secretary of Tiverton Dramatic Society from 1954 until her death eighteen years later. Dotey was involved with every single production -comedy, farce or straight play, either acting, front of house, prompting, doing publicity or supervising refreshments. My brother Jeff and I were often roped in to assist in some capacity, usually behind the scenes, but occasionally also treading the boards. Dotey was one of the few women in Tiverton at that time to produce plays, (the Dramatic Society having then only three women producers), and she made an excellent job of it. At the party following the last night of the successful production of "Barefoot in the Park," the cast had presented her with a bouquet. When she arrived home late in the evening, she found the house in total darkness and thought my father had gone to bed, but he was waiting behind the door in the dark hallway, to knock her and the flowers to the floor as she came in. He was jealous of the popularity and the success she enjoyed in a sphere where he could not touch her. At home, he could degrade and abuse her with impunity, as there were then no laws against domestic violence, but her achievements in the outside world must therefore be punished as soon as she re-entered her home, her prison.

No-body could help, there were no refuges, and the Police in those days would not intervene in what was termed a 'domestic' matter. Jeff once ran to the police station and appealed to them for help, but they declined to assist.

My most cherished memory of Dotey onstage was when she appeared in a play entitled "A Letter From The General", which was, unusually for her, a straight play. Dotey's character in "A Letter From The General" was Sister Magdalene, an elderly nun, living in a remote mission somewhere in the Far East during the Second World War. In the play, the nuns are all granted safe conduct out of the country, but Sister Magdalene gives up her visa to a dissident young priest whom the authorities want to arrest. He disguises himself in her habit and escapes with the nuns, leaving Sister Magdalene alone facing certain death when the soldiers arrive. Dotey gave a tear-jerking performance, the memory of which brings a lump to my throat even now.

My mother's cousins were even keener on am-dram, and appeared in various operatic and theatrical productions in Plymouth, which we were occasionally able to attend. It was always a great treat to go down to see them treading the boards, and I especially recall a production of 'Carousel' with my cousin Elizabeth dancing the part of Louise. She went on to marry the well-known actor Dermot Walsh; sadly, both are now dead, but their daughter, also called

Elizabeth, has carried on the family tradition, becoming a professional actress.

As for me, after the success of "Love on The Dole" I joined a local youth theatre group, which put on modern works such as Harold Pinter's "Night School", in which I played the sweet young woman who was a games mistress by day and, as it turned out, a night-club hostess after school hours. I also took part in "Billy Liar", "Separate Tables" and "The Diary of Anne Frank", but retired from the amateur stage at age eighteen, not having my mother's gift for comedy and being thereafter content with back-stage roles such as prompt or props. I could never be a performer these days as I don't think I could ever hope to remember my lines; yet, strangely, when I go with James Habergham to see "Wild Goose Chase" I find I can recall the words of the dotty archaeologist, which had been my mother's part all those years ago. Memory does play the strangest tricks.

Chapter 25

So much for me not having any African women to stay, as I am about to offer hospitality to Dikeledi, who befriended us in Botswana. She has phoned from Leeds, where she is visiting relations, asking to come for the weekend. She will have to stay in Robin's room for a couple of nights, while he has the settee; Nick will have to sleep on the floor or return to his mother's. (Nick has thought up a new game-show, set in our house, called 'I'm a lodger, get me out of here.') It is quite complicated running a boarding house, organising beds, linen, blankets, towels and food. We never seem to have quite enough.

Dikeledi has chosen the wrong time of year to leave Southern Africa, as the weather is presently very chilly in West Yorkshire. She shivers as she gets into the car, so, instead of driving immediately back to Berringden Brow, we take her to the Tropical House in Roundhay Park where at least she can warm herself, as well as admiring the exotic flora and fauna. (These are of course less of a novelty to her, used as she is to coming face-to-face with a chameleon on her way to the shops, than to the majority of Leeds residents.) Eventually, after a good look round and a hot drink at the café, we have to brave the elements and return home to the chilly Pennines. Dikeledi and Robin exchange news of mutual friends in Botswana, while I cook supper.

This is served in the sitting room rather than the kitchen, so that Dikeledi does not have to move from the fireside. Her feet are still cold, despite me lending her a pair of thick socks, so Robin runs round filling hot water bottles for her. I hope the bottles do not leak, as they are old and hardly ever used, I have had to rummage in the cupboard under the sink and clean off spiders and dust before allowing Robin to fill them. He of course empathises with our guest, as he has suffered considerably from the cold since returning from Africa. Anyone going from the southern summer to the northern winter is bound to find it more of a shock than from the southern winter to the northern summer.

The following day, Dikeledi wants to go shopping. I have never even been in some of the chain stores in Berringden, as I dress myself from charity shops, market stalls, and a wonderful little boutique in the Cloth Hall, which has the most amazing bargains in clothes and footwear. (Frank always told me, rather unkindly I thought, that my dislike of shopping showed. He was a chain store customer, having to take Mother to the White Rose retail centre whenever her agoraphobia permitted; but I prefer a bargain, even if it is last season's style. The wonderful thing about living close to Hebden Bridge is that you can wear what you want, especially if it is something vaguely ethnic; and usually people have far more interesting things to talk about than dress fads and fashions.

After an afternoon in the precinct, we traipse back with various packages and bags, (good job Dikeledi has brought both Robin and me along as Sherpas). It feels very strange to be walking straight past the library, but I would never manage to get through the turnstile with all the packages. At home, I discover a message from James Habergham on the answer-machine, telling me he will be in Hebden Bridge reviewing an event this evening, and asking if he can sleep on my couch rather than driving all the way back to Brighouse. What **is** it with these men, all queuing up to sleep on my couch? I'll have to turn the shed into a bunk-house at this rate. I ring James and explain that we are fully booked this evening. In any case, it is not really far to drive back to Brighouse.

Later, Dikeledi takes me aside and whispers that her period has arrived unexpectedly early. I rush round to the local shop to buy the necessary. She thanks me, then gives me her washing to do. Robin is of course again on hot water bottle detail. I recall that at home, Dikeledi has a maid, a role that I appear to have temporarily assumed. Tired out, we all retire early.

Chapter 26

In the library, I find a number of fliers advertising a community radio station, Berringden Broadcasting, which has a franchise for a month. Scanning the schedule, I realise that Ben is about to take to the airwaves, presenting two hours of movie music each week on Friday evenings. Just how many people will be staying in to listen to that, I wonder …Besides, I am meant to be going to another amateur dramatic performance with James Habergham this Friday.

Back home, I attempt to tune my ancient radio to the wavelength advertised, only to discover that it is practically off the dial. I prance around the living room with the aerial, trying to pick up the signal, and find that in order to have any chance of hearing Berringden Broadcasting it seems to be necessary to stand in the middle of the room, stretching to my full height on tip-toes, with the aerial held aloft, like some sort of cheer-leader frozen in mid cheer. Perhaps last year, at the height of my crush, I might actually have been prepared to do it; but nowadays I would not allow the thought of missing Ben's programme to disturb my hard-won serenity.

Then on Friday, James rings me, full of apologies, to say that he has muddled up the dates, and that the am-dram production is next week. So it seems that I will be at home this evening after all. After tea, Alex asks if he can borrow my old music centre, as it has a deck for playing vinyl records, and he has just discovered a cache of old ones in the loft.

"But I want to listen to 'The Archers' at seven."

"You can borrow my ghetto blaster! It's just that I can't use it, 'cos its got a CD player, and I need a record deck. We'll swap."

"Well OK, I'll be in your room just for tonight, and you can use the front room."

This is a great sacrifice on my part, as no-one in their right mind would really want to exchange the comfort of my front room for the squalor of Alex's bedroom. No wonder Alex readily accepts, and goes to fetch the records.

Upstairs, I switch on Alex's radio and discover that the signal is much clearer here, either because of the location, or perhaps the fact that this is a much newer machine than the one downstairs. After 'The Archers' I twiddle with the dial, and to my amazement find a jingle advertising Berringden Broadcasting, followed by Ben's voice trailing his movie music programme, due to hit the airwaves in half an hour. I decide to listen after all, but after ten minutes I have to say that Ben's musical taste and mine do not really coincide. I would probably have chosen a good selection of classical pieces used as film themes, the Mozart concerto from 'Out of Africa', the Beethoven Piano Sonata used in 'Immortal Beloved,' - you get the general idea. Ben, on the other hand, has chosen scores from films I have never seen, in fact, the only piece I have even heard of is one by Ry Cooder. However, I do not blame Ben for not compiling this week's programme with me in mind. Then Ben announces a competition after the news, the prize being two free cinema tickets.

At this point Robin arrives home. "What on earth are you doing up here?"

"Shush, I'm listening to Ben's programme. There's a competition in a minute."

Ben's voice is heard welcoming listeners back after the news bulletin. I cannot help wondering how many, or few, of us there might be. Ben chatters away for a few minutes, sounding just like he does in the library, quiet in tone and with the odd dry joke interspersed. Then he plays the Noel Harrison tune 'The Windmills Of Your Mind' from the original version of 'The Thomas Crown Affair' and announces the competition question, which is: "What is the name of the actress who played the lead in the remake of the film?"

I know the answer is Renee Rousso, so ring Berringden Broadcasting and leave my details with the receptionist.

Alex appears, having heard the' Windmills Of Your Mind ' tune, saying it is strange, but he has just been playing the same song downstairs, as he has found it among the old 45 rpm vinyl records. I remember it was quite popular when the film came out, all those years ago. By this time, I am fairly desperate to go to the loo, and eagerly await the next advertising break, since I dare not go while Ben is on air in case I miss the competition result. I rush to the bathroom, only to discover the door locked, with Robin is ensconced therein. I cannot possibly hang on until the next batch of adverts, so when Robin emerges, I ask him to keep guard at the radio while I run to the loo. He complains, telling me to be quick, as he has to sort his laundry. I dash back upstairs just as Ben announces that the competition winner is Jess Greenwood, and I cheer so loudly that Alex puts his head round the door again to complain. On hearing that I have won Ben's competition, Alex starts enumerating the films he wants to see, none of which appeal to me in the least. Robin reappears, carrying an armful of his dirty laundry.

"Hello, old bird, are you doing any washing tomorrow? I've a few bits here."

"Oh Robin, why can't you do your own washing! You're here all day!"

"Don't know how to work the machine, old bird, and anyway, you're so much better at it than I am - and you do Alex's for him. Now, whites or coloureds?"

"Coloureds," I reply. "It's the red card for you, I'm afraid, Robin."

Chapter 27

"Alex, where are you roller-blades? I haven't seen you on them for a while."

"Dunnow," shrugs Alex.

"But when was the last time you had them? Did you lend them to someone who forgot to return them?"

Until quite recently, roller-blading was very popular, and I had bought Alex a good pair for his birthday. He had been to blading arenas all over West Yorkshire with his friends. Nowadays, a different set of friends call for him, and none of them appears to be interested in blading. Then I realise that Alex has nothing. He does a paper-round but never has anything to show for it, and the birthday money his godparents gave him seems to have disappeared. He has not spent it on decent clothes, or hi-fi equipment or on a good bike. He hasn't even got a mobile phone, even though they are currently all the rage.

"What do you spend your money on?"

"I dunnow, Mum, it just fucking goes. Will you stop hassling me? It's my money, I can spend it as I choose."

"Don't use language like that!"

"Well, stop giving me all this grief! You're doing my head in!" Alex storms out of the room. He soon reappears, saying that he is going out to meet Kenny.

"Don't you want your tea?"

"Nope." And off he goes. Alex is getting quite chubby, even though he seldom eats his tea. I decide to investigate. I find that the floor of his room is littered with discarded biscuit and sweet wrappers and takeaway cartons. So that's it. He is eating junk food instead of proper meals. What a waste of money.

I hear the back door, Alex coming back. "Forgot my jumper."

"Alex, why do you waste money on junk food? You know I always have tea ready at six o'clock, and if you want a snack there's always fruit and salad."

"Oh, you've been sneaking about in my room, have you? You c...!"

"How dare you use language like that to me in my house!"

"Well, I won't be in the house much longer, cos me and Kenny are off to live in the woods. I've come for my tent and some warm clothes."

I let him go. After all, I can't prevent him, he is so much stronger than me. And maybe a spell in the cold damp woods will do him good. I figure that, after a few nights in a tent with Kenny, home-life with me may seem more appealing.

Alex returns home in the middle of the following morning.

"Hello Alex. That didn't last long," I observe.

" I've come home for a crap, and anyway, some arsehole's set fire to the tent."

"Heavens, Alex, not with you in it!"

"No, of course not. Do I look burned? No, we went to Kenny's place for some breakfast, and when we looked out of his back window the tent was on fire."

"Are you sure you didn't leave a camp fire still smouldering or a cigarette burning?"

"No, and in any case there's a stink of petrol. Now I want Nick's tent. Do we still have it?"

"No, he took it back home," I lie, not wanting Nick's tent set on fire as well. I must remember to hide it away in my wardrobe under a pile of old jumble.

"In that case, we'll make a bender, Kenny's got some old plastic sheeting which his Mum's new sofa came wrapped in. We'll use that."

I tell Alex I am most unhappy about having him sleeping in a bender when there is an arsonist at large. I go down to the woods beside the Berringden Beck, and quickly locate the heap of charred material which had been the tent, sleeping bag and rucksack. Sure enough, there is a strong smell of petrol. I decided to inform the police. They respond quickly, and while they are busily studying the ashes and searching the wood for clues, Alex reappears.

"Lad, you're not to sleep out in these woods. Understand? It's too dangerous. This has obviously been done deliberately. It's lucky you and your mate were not still inside. We'll be keeping a close eye on the area, so no benders or bivouacs. You're too young to leave home anyway. Which is your mate's house? That one over there? We'll be telling his mother the same thing."

Alex returns home with me and asks if I have any rubbish sacks. He looks quite relieved to be home again, and spends the rest of the day tidying up his room, bringing down three large bin-bags of dross from his room. Then at tea-time I find him rummaging in the kitchen cupboards.

"Got any tuna?"

I assume he must be getting together supplies for another woodland sojourn.

"Alex, you're not going back to the woods!"

"Course I'm not! I'm going to make that cheesy pasta tuna thing for tea, to save you cooking."

Chapter 28

James Habergham is due to review an amateur production of a murder mystery, and invites me to meet him in the bar at seven o'clock for a pre-performance drink. I arrive on time, but there is no sign of James. I sit and do the crossword in the local paper, but James still does not arrive. I go outside to look for him, but there is no sign. Now there is an announcement for people to take their seats in the auditorium, so I phone James's mobile. He sounds surprised to hear from me.

"James – where are you? The play's about to begin!"

"The play – oh, yes; I'll be there in about twenty minutes."

I get all the best dates, this one appears to have forgotten all about me, not to mention the review. I suppose I had better take good notes and write it myself. I find I am seated next to the Mayor's consort, who kindly lends me a pen, as a quick scrabble in my handbag reveals that I have come without one – not that I was expecting to have to write anything. Halfway through the first act, James appears, tip-toeing heavily past the Mayor's consort to take his seat.

"Good thing you rang me, Jess," he whispers, "I had completely forgotten."

Of course, in the interval he has to ask me what he missed, but I am possibly the worst person to ask about murder mysteries, as I find it hard to follow intricate plots, and this one appears to be especially convoluted. Since James has missed some vital scene-setting I doubt he will be able to follow a thing. Anyway, as far as I can make out, it seems that the plot hinges on whichever twin was born earlier, and the fact that the clocks go back near Hallowe'en. I provide James with a garbled account, the best I can manage; that will hopefully teach him not to forget a date with me in future.

Frank 's Mother has still not been discharged from hospital, and Frank wants me to visit her again. I agree with reluctance, not especially looking forward to another debate about bed-jackets; but am fortunately spared any such small-talk concerning night attire on this occasion, since Mother sleeps throughout most of our visit. She really is not doing at all well, and I know that Frank is very concerned about her. We are having a spell of fine winter weather, and as we leave the hospital Frank suggests a walk in the nearby country park.

We follow paths through woods and around a lake getting progressively more lost, until we notice a large house on an island. Crossing a bridge, we realise that it is actually a hotel, with an attached health club, so enter the foyer with relief, in the hope of obtaining directions back to where we have left the car. I am also glad to use the loo, and would have appreciated a cup of tea in the cafe, but realise that as it will soon be dark, we had better not linger.

We are told by the helpful receptionist to cross the golf course and follow a wall, which will bring us back to the car-park. Frank and I duly cross the golf course in the gathering gloom, and follow what we hope is the correct wall, only to find, as we reach the top of the hill, that we are walking back towards the lake. The hotel, on its island, can be seen not far away. By this time it is dusk, and I tell Frank that I am going to return to the hotel and call a taxi. Luckily, I have ten pounds on me. Frank demurs, saying that we should give the golf course route another try; but being cold, tired, muddy, thirsty, hungry, and also, I have to admit, rather scared, I have had quite enough. We part company, with me deciding to call it a day, and rather resenting Frank's lack of chivalry in not escorting me back to the hotel; while Frank equally despises my lack of backbone in giving up our quest for the car-park. Entering the welcoming warmth of the hotel foyer, I glance back to see Frank disappearing over the crest of the hill. I then explain my predicament to the receptionist, just as a small, rather elderly man emerges from the health club door carrying a kit bag. He has evidently caught the tail end of my story.

"Where do you want to be, love, 'cos I've got my car outside, and I'll give you a lift if you want. I'm heading towards Fitzwilliam, if that's any help."

"Well, yes, that is the right direction. I'd like a lift, if it's not too much trouble."

I do not usually accept lifts from strangers, but feel that if he is a member of the health club in these opulent surroundings, presumably someone here has had to vouch for him. Besides, he has a kind face, not that this is much to go on. The man strides nimbly down the path, and ushers me to a red Mercedes.

"Get in love. You'll be quite safe with me"

I am hesitating, concerned not so much about his probity but about my muddy shoes in this lovely car.

"My shoes – they're filthy!"

"Not to worry, I've got something." He rummages in his bag and produces two plastic bags for me to wrap round my feet, so I sink back into the comfort of the passenger seat, prepared to relax and admire the rapidly darkening wintry scenery. During the journey, the old gentleman tells me he is a retired miner, a widower, who likes to keep himself fit, so he goes to the health club to swim most days. In almost no time at all I am back in Frank's village, and outside Frank's house but there is no sign of Frank's car, or indeed of Frank, and his house is in darkness. Thanking my kind saviour, I emerge from the Mercedes, feet still wrapped in plastic bags, and decide that my best course of action is to see if the neighbours have a key. They do not, but on hearing my sad story, offer me sanctuary and tea until such time as Frank should return. Talk about the kindness of strangers…I am on my second cup when I notice Frank's car drawing up, followed immediately by a taxi. Frank dashes into his house, keeping the taxi waiting, then reappears with his wallet and pays the fare. I thank the neighbours for their hospitality and run round to Frank's house to find out what happened to him after he left me at the hotel.

It turns out that he went around the golf course again, and this time followed a different wall, but still inexplicably ended up back at the hotel. It all seemed rather like Alice in Wonderland. Frank was not as lucky as I had been, there was no helpful health club patron emerging from the changing rooms, and he had therefore been obliged to call a taxi. (This was, I remind him, my original plan.) But of course, it had been me who had the ten pound note, Frank had no money on him. The taxi had delivered him to the car-park, which is normally locked up at dusk, in fact the barrier was just about to be lowered, and he had narrowly escaped having his vehicle locked in overnight. The taxi-man had followed Frank home in order to collect his fare, and the whole sorry escapade had ended up costing Frank twelve pounds fifty – rather a lot to pay for lack of chivalry, I feel, since of course, had he done the decent thing and stayed with me he would have had a free ride home in a Mercedes.

I rather feel like crowing and telling him it serves him right, but settle instead for an expression of quiet amusement, punctuated by the occasional giggle.

Frank looks extremely cross, as he is cold, tired, hungry, thirsty and poorer by twelve pounds fifty, whereas I, in contrast, am warm, rested and refreshed. Franks puts a pizza in the oven for supper, and I offer to help him by making a salad. By the time we sit down to eat, Frank's mood has improved somewhat, and he starts to tell me about a lady named Elaine, a new member of his Tuesday dance group, whom he describes as being gorgeous with long blonde hair and a voluptuous figure. He confides that he has always wanted to go out with a blonde, and hopes to have the opportunity of asking her out next week, providing he can get her away from her rather plain friend for long enough to strike up a conversation.

"Why do these pretty women always have an unattractive friend dogging their every footstep?" complains Frank. I cheerfully suggest that it is probably to protect them from the unwanted attentions of men like him, and reassure him that Elaine will lose the friend soon enough if she is at all interested.

Chapter 29

There is a Health Fair this Saturday in Berringden Leisure Centre. I look round the stalls, picking up information about various diseases from which I hope never to suffer; then I receive a free massage from a man who has set up some beds in the corner. Actually, it is some sort of manipulation rather than massage, and is quite refreshing. Finally, I find myself at a stall dealing with health matters for young people, staffed by a friendly looking young man, with a number of leaflets on the table in front of him. I browse through them, not sure exactly what I am looking for, and, sensing my hesitation, the young man asks if he can help.

"What sort of young people's illicit activities involve the use of plastic bottles?" I enquire. "Only my garden is always full of them, and so is the shed."

The young man picks up a booklet on cannabis, and shows me a page where something called a 'bong' is described and illustrated. It is apparently constructed out of plastic bottles to form a sort of hubble- bubble device.

"It intensifies the effect of the drug," explains the young man. "In any case, cannabis today is much stronger than it used to be. It 's been implicated in schizophrenia in some recent studies. And of course it's a great de-motivator."

When I was a student, we always used to be told that cannabis was not especially harmful – not that I ever tried it, I don't care for smoking anything, but the impression given by various acquaintances was that the tobacco in the joint, spliff, roach, or whatever it was called, was more harmful than the actual cannabis. In fact, the medicinal properties of cannabis were often extolled. People to whom I have expressed my concerns regarding Alex usually say 'Well, if its only cannabis' as if it is something quite harmless, simply giving you the munchies and making you giggle. But it seems from this information leaflet that it is mentally addictive and far more dangerous than I imagined.

I retire to the tea tables and sit down soberly. So much has now been finally explained. Alex's complete lack of interest in schoolwork, his 'can't be arsed' attitude to life in general. The disappearance of his roller-blades – sold to buy dope, I suppose - and the fact that all his paper-round, Christmas and birthday money goes without him having anything to show for it. The theft of the gas money from my purse. The strange-looking kids who call for him, the late night unexplained phone-call – could it be a drug dealer? The junk food consumed when he has had the munchies after smoking, the plastic bottles and strange smells, and the running water – these are all used for the bongs. That outside tap must be like a honey-pot attracting kids from miles around. I must have it disconnected, Of course, this won't stop them using cannabis, it will simply drive the problem elsewhere, to another garden with an outside tap and not overlooked at the back, but hopefully, I will be able to move within the next few months, as soon as the housing association receives its new budget.

As if to confirm my worst suspicions, when I return home I find the shed with dense clouds of smoke issuing from the window. Glancing in, I can just about make out Alex and Kenny in the middle of the swirling scented fumes, bending over one of the plastic bottle contraptions.

"Whatever are you doing? You'll have us all arrested!" I rush into the shed, as Alex and Kenny look up in amazement.

"Chill out, Mum, I'm just pulling Kenny a bong."

I do not remember much of what happens after that. My mental health seems to have been deteriorating for some time, and has now become too fragile. I simply cannot cope. I scream, I shout, I curse. I frighten the cat and disturb the neighbours. I am beside myself with anger. I am choking with rage. I am shaking. I am incoherent. Kenny legs it, while Alex looks non-plussed.

"Mum, don't have a f…ing spazz attack! Listen, I'll make you a cup of tea."

I gather whatever strength I have and throw the bong contraption at him. Water goes everywhere, and fresh clouds of strange-smelling smoke pervade the atmosphere of Berringden Brow.

"Get out, Alex, get out of my house. You don't deserve to live here!"

"OK, OK, I'll go. But Mum, it's only weed. It's nothing heavy!"

But it's too much for me to bear.

What does a woman in my situation do? I feel I need to talk to someone, so ring my brothers Jeff in Devon and Peter in Hampshire. They are of course sympathetic but feel they are geographically too far away to be of any practical help. Then I ring Jim the vicar, who say he will come straight round.

"Would it help if I had a word with Alex?" asks Jim, over a cup of tea. I thank him for the offer, but I know Alex has gone off religion since the removal of the previous vicar, Kev the Rev, to Northumberland a few years ago. Sadly, at the very same time, Tony the Scout master, whom Alex liked and admired, died very suddenly at the age of fifty. Alex, who had been in the church companies of the Beavers, Cubs and Scouts since the age of six, lost two men who had been important to him just as he was approaching puberty, obviously a critical time in any lad's life. Meanwhile, Jim is concerned that I should see the doctor, so I make an appointment on Monday. (Our doctors are marvellous, we never have to wait long as with some practices.) Dr. Jones is sympathetic, but says that he can do nothing about Alex's drug-taking unless Alex himself asks for it. He confirms that cannabis is mentally addictive, and that there is always the danger that those who use it heavily may move on to a harder drug, since he says that those who deal in cannabis often have contacts with hard drug dealers. He offers me anti-depressants; but I am not keen to take tablets when the cause of my present distress and anxiety is not located within me, but is directly attributable to another person's behaviour.

I am also extremely concerned about the legal implications for myself – isn't there a law about not allowing one's premises to be used for the consumption of drugs? Could I be prosecuted for unknowingly allowing my shed to become the Berringden Brow bong centre?

It occurs to me that I could speak to someone at Alex's school, not the form teacher whom he despises, but the Head of English, whom he has always liked. Unfortunately, Mr. Gardner does not teach Alex this year, but says he will try to get hold of him for a quiet chat. At least Alex attends school, even though he does next to no work but simply dreams the days away.

Since the precipitate departure of Alex's oceanographer father to work in New Zealand before he was even born, I have tried to be everything to him, parent, guardian, protector, teacher, guide, friend, financer - but I'm not superwoman. He is clearly too much for me to cope with, but who is willing and able to help? Clergymen, teachers and doctors can offer moral support, but not much more.

I recall the old African saying, "It takes a village to raise a child", which may still hold good in traditional societies but is probably not really applicable here in Britain nowadays, where society is much more individualistic. I try to remember how I dealt with Tom's bad behaviour as a teenager, but really it did not amount to much. I recall ringing the Samaritans one night after Tom had lost his temper following a drunken teenage party, to tell them about a broken window and a smashed kitchen chair. The Samaritan lady was very good, she listened patiently to my lengthy tirade, after which I felt much better. On seeing how upset I was, Tom was full of contrition, his father Bill came and mended the chair, and Tom behaved himself ever after. Funnily enough, I remember that Alex, then eight years old, had also interceded with me on behalf of his elder brother. It made such a difference, having someone else in the house to help diffuse the tension, but now there is no-one else here. Both the lodgers are away, Robin visiting friends in the Midlands and Nick spending a rare week at his mother's. These men are never around when I need them.

Three days pass, and I have mixed feelings. While it is very good for me to have time to myself and not to have someone calling me a c… every five minutes, I still feel that I should have tried harder to help Alex through this phase. The trouble is that I simply do not have the resources, the strength and energy and robust mental health required for such a task. And at present I do not even know where he is, although he is likely to be staying locally with a friend – at least, I hope that is the case. While I feel that I had to throw him out of the house in order to preserve my own sanity, I do not really like the idea of a homeless teenager roaming the February streets. And if and when Alex does return, I do not want the same old cycle of drink and drugs and offensive language to begin all over again, yet I am at a loss to know how to prevent it.

I suddenly realise that Tuesday is Pancake Day. Alex loves pancakes and I feel sure he will come home then. I need to devise some sort of strategy so that I am prepared for his arrival. No-one I have spoken to so far, while all are sympathetic, has been able to provide me with constructive advice on how to deal with Alex. Later however I have a brain-wave. Until he started with this disaffected 'can't be arsed' phase, Alex was a regular member of the local youth club. Indeed, he had been the young person representative on the management committee. Maybe I should ring the leader, Ian, since he must have had a great deal of experience in dealing with lads such as Alex. I dial his number and am about to explain what has happened, when Ian stops me.

"I know a bit about what's been going off at your house."

"You know? How do you know?"

"I've seen your lad next door at Kenny's, and he told me what happened. He's stopping at Kenny's just now, sleeping on the floor. From what he's said, I think he's right sorry about upsetting you like he did.

I've told him to come back to Youth Club if he wants, and he said he'd think about starting again next Wednesday."

Goodness, it takes a village, even here in Berringden Brow...

"Oh, do you meet on Wednesdays now? He used to go on Sundays."

"Still is on Sundays for the Seniors, but Alex felt he'd outgrown the Sunday sessions, and I want him to come on Wednesdays to help out with the Juniors. He's got real skills, your lad, even though he's been acting daft lately and you might not think so. He can help us with the ten and eleven year olds."

"Do you really think so? But won't he be a bad influence on them, what with smoking dope and cigarettes - and what about the drink and the language?"

"I guarantee that while he's at Club there will be no bad behaviour of any kind. And I've spoken to Alex about his use of drugs, he knows it's not clever."

"Well, it certainly sounds as is it's worth a try, Ian. Thanks for all your help."

"That's OK. I think he's getting ready to come home and apologise, see if you'll have him back."

I tell Ian that I confidently expect him through the door at tea-time on Pancake Day, Shrove Tuesday, and reflect that if ever there was a boy who needed to be shriven, it is Alex, although the religious significance of Shrovetide will no doubt be quite lost on him.

Chapter 30

I receive a worrying email from my friend Sehlile in Zimbabwe. Things are getting very difficult there, with political unrest and severe food shortages. It is apparently becoming almost impossible to get essential items such as cooking oil, sugar and maize meal without queuing or resorting to the black market or even going to neighbouring countries to buy them.

Sehlile is lucky in that she at least still has a job, working for an international distribution company in Bulawayo, the city where I met her when we were on our African trip. Sehlile helped me by staying with me, a complete stranger, when Nick and Alex became lost on a shopping trip in Bulawayo. Eventually, after I had spent an anxious morning waiting for them at the appointed rendez-vous in the heat, Alex and Nick turned up, safe and sound and quite unconcerned, and Sehlile and I have stayed in touch ever since. The following day, an official from the Housing Association arrives. He makes me a definite offer in line with the market value of the house, and tells me to go ahead immediately and look for another property, with a view to moving early in the new financial year. This is music to my ears, as I will soon be able to get away from the bongs, the druggies, the shed, the fence, the rampant plants, disgruntled neighbours, bogus council officials and everything else which has recently contributed to my poor state of health.

At four o'clock on Shrove Tuesday Alex arrives on the doorstep and asks if he can come in. I tell him I have a plate of pancakes keeping warm in the oven. Alex eats his tea in silence. When he has finished he turns to me.

"Well, then, can I come home?"

"That depends on whether you're prepared to abide by my conditions."

"Which are?"

"You must give up all use of drugs, and your bad language, and cut right back on your smoking and drinking."

"I already have. I'll fetch my stuff from Kenny's and be back in half an hour."

"One more thing – I never want to hear the words 'I can't be arsed' again."

I notice that Alex has not yet apologised to me for the distress his behaviour has caused, but decide to wait a while. At least he appears willing to try to mend his ways, and his manner seems subdued; evidently the experience of being homeless and having to sleep on Kenny's floor has given him something to think about. And I suspect that his talk with Ian about helping at the Junior Youth Club has helped a lot. At first, I was not sure exactly what skills and abilities Alex might have to offer the local ten and eleven year olds, but I suppose he can organise football games. If he has really decided to come out of his disaffected phase and behave in a more constructive manner then there is hope.

When Alex returns with his rucksack he goes straight to his room. I hear him clattering about, then he calls down the stairs asking if I have a spare bin-bag.

Empty bottles, beer cans, discarded cigarette packets and even a bedraggled cannabis plant are bagged up and taken out to the dustbin. Alex then borrows the Hoover and returns upstairs In the middle of all this, Robin reappears unannounced, back from his visit to old friends in Sedgley.

"Helping your Mum with the Spring cleaning, Al? Good lad. You could pass the Hoover over that carpet in my room after you've finished in yours…and have you washed my sheets while I've been away, old bird? I think I must be due some clean ones. I suppose there are no pancakes left? Thought not. Oh well, maybe some cheese on toast? No cheese? Dear me, this is a poor homecoming. I suppose it had better be the chip shop again…"

I suddenly realise that another advantage of moving house will be that it presents an ideal opportunity for getting rid of demanding lodgers.

I visit Hebden Bridge to look at estate agents. As I had feared, there is nothing in the town within my price range, but there is a property in the neighbouring village of Heptonroyd, which I feel might suit me. The owner, an elderly lady has moved into sheltered accommodation. Her house has a lovely view at the front, which compensates somewhat for the lack of central heating and the fact that the bathroom is on the landing, which I feel is a somewhat unusual arrangement. The agent tells me that this was in fact fairly common in the area, as people did not want to sacrifice a bedroom when they installed indoor bathrooms. I put in an offer, reflecting that I can always alter the arrangement of the rooms if I manage to buy the house. The fact that there is no garden, only a back yard, is a bonus as far as I am concerned, as there are no out-of-control climbing plants to deal with and no grass to trigger off my hay fever as I struggle to mow it. I ask the agent if she has heard of any problems with drug users locally, whereupon she shakes her head, looking faintly horrified.

Chapter 31

Robin is not very pleased at the prospect of having to leave. I tell him that I will have fewer bedrooms at the new house, after the bathroom has been moved from the landing, and so there will be no room for him. Besides, he has been back in the UK for six months, quite long enough to sort himself out.

"So you're making me homeless now – why don't you evict Alex again, he's caused you more grief than I ever have."

"Alex is my teenage son, you are over sixty. I have a duty to house Alex until he is eighteen, and the council has a duty to accommodate you, as an older person. That's the law." I do not mention the fact that Robin caused me a huge amount of grief when he left for Africa five and a half years ago, as it does not seem worth arguing about the matter. Besides, Alex is really making an effort these days. He even has a job arranged for half term week, helping Kenny's father dig a drainage trench at a house in the village. Alex will use the money earned to pay off his drug debt to the creepy late-night phone caller, who as I suspected, is a dope dealer. I am very pleased that the debt will soon be settled. Alex owes £50, which represents ten sixteenths-of-an-ounce portions of cannabis. Alex explains that an ounce of the stuff costs £60, but when divided up, each sixteenth costs proportionately more, so that in fact the dealers make £20 per ounce, since sixteen £5s are £80. Alex is never any good at problems involving weight and money when set for Maths homework, but he appears to be able to work out these sums relating to dope in a trice…

I am still fairly horrified to think that my son has been mixing with drug dealers in the back streets of Hebden Bridge, a place I love to visit for reasons completely unconnected with illegal substances. The cinema, the theatre, the market, the charity shops, the pubs and cafes where I meet my friends, the riverside walks, the spectacular scenery and bluebells of Hardcastle Crags, the Plot Night Bonfire, plus the annual arts festival, are what takes me to the town; (you should go there, too, if you haven't been already.)

On Wednesday night, Alex goes to help Ian at the Junior Youth Club, and now he tells me they are planning to be away on a trip to a hostel in the Dales at the weekend. It so happens that Frank has invited me to someone's fiftieth birthday party dance, also in Wharfedale, so I suggest that we stay in a nearby Bed and Breakfast and make a weekend of it, rather than drive back home in the darkness of a freezing February night. Of course we will have separate rooms – this would have applied even if we had still been close, since Frank is a light sleeper and I snore heavily. The pub in the village where the party is to be held says it can accommodate us, and all is arranged.

Then, the day before we are due to go away, Frank rings to tell me it is all off, as he is taking Elaine, the woman he fancies from the Tuesday dance group, instead. He says she rang him and asked him to go over to her house, ostensibly to look over some dances they were calling at the next meeting.

"But one thing led to another, and I ended up staying the night," says Frank, adding, "The sex was tempestuous!" My first feeling on hearing this news is of astonishment that people still use these hackneyed phrases outside the agony columns of the tabloid newspapers, but then I feel annoyed, not because he has found a new love, but because it messes up the plans for the weekend, and I will now have to cancel the B and B. booking at short notice, What if they make me pay? Frank and Elaine do not want the reservation as he says she has friends nearby with whom they can stay.

Luckily for me, the landlady is sympathetic, and says she will not require payment, but I am still cross, as I now have nothing to do this weekend, even though Alex is away and it would have been a good opportunity for me to take a short break. I feel rather despondent until I suddenly remember the monastery in Lancashire where we had once spent a wonderful Parish weekend, in the days when Kev the Rev was the vicar, before he left for Corbridge-on-Tyne. I know they take weekend visitors, not necessarily in parish groups, but people on their own who just want to be quiet. I find I still have the number in my old address book, so ring and explain that I am looking for somewhere tranquil to spend this coming weekend.

Sister Agatha answers. "Oh dear, we are fully booked this weekend. There is a large group coming, and all the rooms are taken – oh, except one tiny single room in one of the cottages."

"Well, please may I have that?"

"Yes, if you wish; but it is **very** small."

"That's absolutely fine by me."

Sister Agatha starts giving me directions to the monastery, but I tell her that this is not necessary, since I have been before, with a parish group.

"Oh, which group was that?"

"From Berringden Brow, several years ago now, when Kevin was our vicar..."

"It's Kevin's new parish which is coming here this weekend. He's bringing a large party from Corbridge-on-Tyne."

"Goodness! What a coincidence!" I can hardly contain my delight.

"Well, God moves in mysterious ways," laughs Sister Agatha.

Chapter 32

The prospect of getting away for a few days is wonderful. Alex departs with the Youth Club in the minibus, and I fling a few things into a bag and drive over to the monastery. I should explain that this particular monastery is run by nuns rather than monks, but is not a convent. I do not really understand why this is; all I know is that it is a lovely place run by caring people. It was at this same time of year that we went before, and the snowdrops were blooming in huge white drifts on the lawn. Sister Agatha receives me kindly, and gives me the keys to my room in the cottage, which is behind the main building. Single people, or those who come on their own are usually put up in the cottage, which was previously quite Spartan and chilly; in fact we had been advised to bring hot-water bottles with us on the previous occasion, not having bed companions to keep us warm. Now the cottage has been renovated and central heating installed. I find my tiny room upstairs, and unpack quickly. Then I set off to find Kev the Rev and his wife Jenny. They are just coming out of the dining room. There are hugs and kisses all round, and I am introduced to the other members of the Corbridge party. There is much smiling and shaking of heads, and Sister Agatha's remark about God moving in mysterious ways is repeated many times. After I have had my supper, I am invited to join them for evening service, and so we all go to the chapel for prayers. I feel very happy.

I do not wish to intrude upon the business part of the Corbridge Parish weekend, so after breakfast the next morning I leave them to their meeting and head for the village. Kev has promised to lead a walk during the afternoon, which I am invited to join if I wish. I smile as I recall the previous occasion, when Kev led us out into the woods and fields, up hills and over dales, in ever diminishing circles in the fast-fading afternoon light, so that the people back at the monastery were quite anxious as to what could have become of us. (No-one had a mobile phone in those days, only a few years ago, strange as this now seems.) We finally made it safely back, after the church-wardens had studied the map, and instructed us all to retrace our steps through the woods and out onto a country lane, after which I wrote a poem for the parish magazine along the lines of those wishing to go for any future walks with Kev being advised to take distress flares, sextants, bivouacs and plenty of Kendal mint-cake. Kev tells me that this afternoon's excursion is only as far as the local bird reserve, so hopefully we will find our way there and back without too much trouble.

Unfortunately, the weather does not look as if it will hold, and by the time we reach the bird hide it is raining steadily and blowing a gale. I peer out from the wooden shelter over the choppy water, and see no sign of any bird life. The birds appear to have sensibly decided to take cover until the weather clears up. Then I notice one solitary bedraggled black specimen bobbing about in the water some distance from the edge of the lake. Kev also spots it.

"Look, it's a **Little Auk!** " he exclaims in great excitement. "They're quite rare."

The bird appears to me, one of the uninitiated so far as bird-watching is concerned, to be totally unremarkable, as it struggles vainly to reach the bank.

"Wait a minute, I don't think it is an Auk; no, it's not," Kev's voice sinks in disappointment as he peers through his binoculars, trying to establish the unfortunate creature's true identity. Then it rises in glee once again.

"It's a **Slovenian Grebe**! How about that! They're fairly unusual here as well!"

The poor bird, quite unaware of all the excitement it is causing amongst the Corbridge Parish weekenders, seems to be in danger of sinking beneath the waves as it drifts further away from the lake shore. Just then another party of twitchers arrives at the hide, also bursting with restrained excitement.

"Have you seen it?" they ask Kev. "That Slovenian Grebe out on the water?"

I imagine the poor bird is wishing it had never left Slovenia, and is even now planning to return at the earliest possible opportunity.

We walk back through the incessant rain, and after dinner, spend a pleasant evening chatting, doing a quiz and playing party games (of the reasonably dignified, rather than raucous variety, as befits our monastic surroundings). I eventually return with my fellow cottage dwellers to our kitchen, where we make tea, and continue the conversation until late. It turns out that one of the Corbridge men used to live in Berringden Brow, his children are about the same ages as mine, and he likes classical music, so we have plenty to talk about. Mysterious ways or coincidence, this has been a wonderful weekend, and I doubt Frank will have had such a good time at the birthday dance as I have had here at the monastery, his tempestuous new love notwithstanding.

Chapter 33

After morning service and Sunday lunch it is time to say goodbye to Kev, Jenny, the kind nuns, and my new friends from Corbridge, and drive home. I arrive back home just before Alex and the Youth Club return. Alex looks exhausted as he gets off the bus. Ian gives him an affectionate slap on the back and tells me Alex has worked hard.

"Those little kids - the tricks they get up to!" Alex shakes his head ruefully.

"Now you know what you mum has been feeling like, with you leading her a merry dance all these years," laughs Ian, as I nod in agreement.

Valentines Day falls this week, but I am not sending any cards, nor do I expect to receive any; so when two envelopes, one pink and one crimson, drop through the letter box I imagine they must be for Alex. To my surprise, both are addressed to me. The pink one is a comical one from Nick, which makes me laugh out loud. Inside the crimson envelope is a card with a picture of two cute love-birds, and in Frank's unmistakable scrawl is the message

"Still missing you."

I smell a rat.

Who would bother to send their old love a Valentine card, having just embarked upon a tempestuous affair with someone else? Come to think of it, who would use the corny old phrase "and one thing led to another"? Only someone who was making the whole thing up, for what reason I know not.

At teatime, I ring Frank. He is in. I ask if he is busy. He says he is not.

"Shouldn't you be preparing a candle-lit supper for Elaine?"

"I'm not seeing her tonight."

"Not seeing your new true love on Valentine's night?"

"No, she'd already arranged to do something else."

"I'm just ringing to ask just how many Valentines cards you've sent this year."

"Oh- only the two."

"And does Elaine know that you also sent me a card?"

"Err, no; but I didn't want you to feel left out now that you don't have anyone to send you a Valentine card."

"How thoughtful, but your current girl-friend might not see it that way, and anyway, your assumption about me is incorrect."

With that, I ring off, unable to suppress my amusement a moment longer and afraid my giggles will give the game away.

I am not altogether surprised when the following day's post brings a letter from Frank, confessing what I already know, that he has made up the whole story about Elaine and one thing leading to a tempestuous other in order to make me jealous He had wanted to get his revenge on me for having ended our rather dreary relationship last year, and for then having taken in Robin. (Heavens, no need for him to be envious – I can easily arrange for him to have Robin as a lodger if he likes.). He had actually fancied Elaine, but she had made it clear that she wanted nothing to do with him. (Sensible woman) He had gone to the dance party alone, but revenge had not tasted as sweet as he had expected (it seems quite impossible for this man to discuss anything without the liberal use of clichés,) and he had not enjoyed it especially, so decided to send me the Valentine card.

Frank should have known that I would have had the intelligence to put two and two together; but then, he is only the latest in a long line of men, to underestimate me, (beginning with my father, who said I would never be able to spell the name Jacqueline, which my mother had chosen for me, but thought I might just manage Jess; and continuing via Bill, who never believed I would get any of my stories or articles published, telling me that I was suffering from 'delusions of grandeur' in even attempting to do so, and advising me to spend more time using the Hoover than the type-writer.)

How am I to respond to this letter? It seems so childish that it scarcely merits a reply; yet it has come from the pen of a fifty-year old man. Seemingly, now he has failed to attract Elaine, or indeed, anyone else, he has decided that he might as well fall back on me – good old Jess, her hair might be starting to go grey, she's a bit plump and not exactly stylish, but she is kind and reliable and still available - is probably his line of thought. He once told me, when we were going out together, that he was only making do with me until something better came along, and I don't think he was joking. Well, I am not really interested in playing games; although I do want him to know that I had a very enjoyable weekend, despite his attempt to ruin it for me, by letting me down at the last moment on the spurious pretext of having found a new girl-friend. However, it seems he succeeded only in cutting off his nose to spite his face (oh, no, the dreaded clichés; he's even got me overdosing on them now, my serenity having deserted me.) I must settle down and compose a suitable reply

I bought a few postcards at the monastery, and decide to send one to Frank:

"Having a good time, beautiful place, wonderful people, surrounded by love. J"

Of course, the sort of love with which I was surrounded at the monastery was not the tempestuous kind, but the constant and sincere love which true friends, both old and new, bear for each other. This post-card does not lie.

Chapter 34

My friend David is holding his annual Pisces party, for those of us lucky enough to be born under the fish sign. We guests must take something to eat, plus some other fishy item, and have been warned that we must be prepared to recount a story, sing a song, or tell a joke, all on the theme of fish. The problem is that of course we cannot take *real* fish as our foodstuff, since David's is a vegetarian household. I inform Ben about this imminent gathering as I search the music library for a fishy song.

"Bet you're glad you're a Cancerian, Ben." Ben nods and manages a smile.

"How are things? I enquire.

"Humph, life's just a long list of things to be done before you die."

Ben is evidently not in the mood for trivial conversation.

After some time pondering what food to take I decide upon a carrot cake with an icing fish decoration. My fishy item is a small drum of fish food flakes, but I have a few qualms as I hand it in to David, since I am not sure what goes into those flakes – is it politically correct vegetarian plankton or something meaty?

In David's kitchen there is a lovely fish-shaped jelly, (set with agar-agar, of course, not animal-derived gelatine), some fish-shaped biscuits, and a bowl of something spicy served in a fish-shaped dish. David takes our coats upstairs. (His wife, being a Virgo, has been banished for the evening.) The fish flakes are accepted and added to the collection of fishy items; so far these include a soap dish, a picture, a book ("The Compleat Angler") and the fish jelly-mould.

I find the rest of my fellow Pisceans assembled around the fire in the living room, discussing the row of shrunken heads dangling from the mantelpiece. David's dissertation, and subsequent book, was about Yorkshire stone heads, so I am not surprised to see these decorations, although they do appear rather grotesque, glinting in the firelight.

One party-goer, Joan, recoils in horror. "Ugh -they-they're not real, are they?"

"I hardly think that's likely in a vegetarian household," Pete sounds reassuring.

But I cannot resist the opportunity to tease. "Well, actually, I think this one's the paperboy, and that's the dustman. And on this side there's the milkman, and next to him there's the postman. And see this one in the middle, that's a very rare specimen, the census enumerator, they only come round once every ten years...and he just needs the window-cleaner to complete the collection."

Joan's expression of horror gives way to a smile as she realises I am joking. Meanwhile, David is serving the food, all of which is delicious. After supper, we have to perform our party pieces. Someone tells a fishy tale, there are a number of fishy jokes, and some fishy songs. I do "Fish gotta swim and birds gotta fly", while David gives us "They swam and swam right over the dam," and Pete sings "Thou shalt have a fishy on a little dishy when the boat comes in."

Joan has produced a fishy word-search, which we settle down to after the excitement of the musical items. We Pisceans know how to enjoy ourselves.

Next day, I go to the library eager to tell Ben about the Pisces party, which he has missed because of his summer birthday, but he forestalls me by reaching under the library counter and producing a book, apparently from the children's literature section, entitled "Jess Greenwood and the Guide Camp Adventure."

"I didn't know they wrote stories about you 'til I saw this in the pile for the next sale of withdrawn books," Ben explains. I notice that it bears a 30p price tag.

"Goodness, I did not know they wrote books about me either; its evidently one of a series," I exclaim, studying the lengthy list of other 'Jess Greenwood' titles inside the back cover, from which it appears that my lucky namesake has had all manner of adventures and been caught up in various excitements and mysteries involving field trips, holidays, school plays and TV quiz shows.

"What an interesting life you lead," Ben comments, looking over my shoulder.

"Should I take this away and read it? Is it an early birthday gift?"

"Do whatever you like with it," says Ben in an amused tone. I decide against insulting him by offering him the 30 pence he must have paid in order to retrieve it from the sale, so smile my thanks and leave.

At home, I am just settling down to read my new book when there is a knock at the front door. I answer it and discover a handsome young man dressed in cycling attire on the doorstep. Needless to say, he is not looking for me, but wants to know whether Sharon is in. I inform him that Sharon does not live here but around the corner

"Are you quite sure she doesn't live here?" the young man queries, attempting to peer past me into the front room, as if he suspects Sharon might be lurking within and I am trying to conceal her. I reiterate that he has the wrong house, whereupon he launches into a lengthy explanation of how he recently met Sharon on a train, since when they have emailed each other several times. She has told him she lives in the Close, in a house with lots of pots and tubs of flowers outside the door, and my house appears to answer this description perfectly. I point out that this is not in fact the Close, but the Avenue, and he really needs to be in the street round the corner. He still does not seem entirely convinced, so I slip my shoes on and escort him around to the Close, indicating Sharon's house; however, she has unfortunately gone out.

Before I can commiserate with the young man and offer him a drink, he appears to read my mind, and hastily jumping onto his bike, pedals away down the hill and onto the main road, with rather more speed than politeness, I feel, considering that I have been good enough to show him the right house.

The only time I get dishy young men knocking on the door for me is when they are selling double-glazing, or dusters for the disabled, or a new type of electricity. Occasionally, it's the Mormons who send handsome young people pedalling their brand of religion, (the Jehovah's witnesses never seem particularly attractive) but I don't invite any of them in. And I've never met anyone on a train and inspired them to dash round to my house on a bike at an early opportunity...I can feel my serenity slipping, so hastily dismiss all such envious thoughts from my mind and carry on reading my book, quite a respectable consolation prize really, since not everyone receives a birthday gift from their favourite librarian.

Chapter 35

I visit the local art club's annual exhibition, as Ben has told me that he is exhibiting two pictures in the 'still life' category. I find the pictures and gaze at them for a few moments. They depict apples and plums; both appear to my uninitiated eye to be perfectly executed, and I especially like the way he has captured the bloom on the fruit. Ben is obviously something of a perfectionist.

While I can admire his skill, the pictures in the exhibition that really appeal to me are the landscapes of the moors above Berringden Brow, in a haze of blue sky, yellow gorse and purple heather. If I was a painter, the beautiful local landscape would be my chosen subject. I notice that nearly all the paintings bear price tags, and Ben's efforts are priced at £70 for the apples and £80 for the plums. I wonder if anyone will buy them. They are actually quite cheap in comparison with the apparently sky-high prices being asked for many of the other paintings. I suppose they must have taken hours to complete, and decide that art is something for which I would never have the patience.

I arrive home to see a jean-clad leg disappearing through the top part of the landing window. Someone has climbed onto the shed roof and is in the act of breaking into the house. I am just about to summon the police on my mobile phone when a face appears at the window and grins cheekily at me. It is Alex's friend Kenny.

"Hi, Jess," he calls from the window. "If we'd known you were right behind we would have come in the front door."

"What on earth do you think you're doing? That's housebreaking! I was just about to call the police."

"Chill, Jess; we're only waiting for Alex."

"We? Who else is there?"

Emma's pretty face appears, shyly smiling. "Hello, Mrs. Greenwood."

"Emma, you should know better than to break into someone's house."

"Alex said you wouldn't mind us coming in and waiting for him…"

"Well, I **do** mind; I'm going to open the door and you can disappear, I never want to see either of you here again. I've a good mind to tell your parents."

The two run off, Kenny muttering about my lack of hospitality. It occurs to me that Alex might behave in the same disreputable manner at friends' houses, so I decide not to phone Kenny and Emma's parents, as who knows what tales they will have to tell me? I still feel mentally fairly fragile, and am able to cope with nothing more complicated than everyday routine stuff. I do not need more rows and arguments. When he comes home, I tell Alex to meet his friends away from the house, as I want to feel safe in my own home. Suppose I had not seen Kenny's leg and had come in to find those two, unexpectedly on the landing? I might have had a heart attack. Alex of course thinks this is wild exaggeration; he seems to think I am making a lot of fuss about nothing.
After all, they had not damaged or taken anything, they wouldn't, as they are sound, good mates, whom he had invited; they simply arrived a little early, and really did not deserve to be turned out of the house in such a fashion.

"Mm, you're mental," says Alex rushing off to find Kenny and Emma, while I start praying that the Housing Association will come up with the money to enable us to move very soon.

Meanwhile, I had better get locks fitted on the landing window. I ring Piscean David, whose lodger, Jez, is a handyman. Jez says he can come the day after tomorrow. I consider getting him to demolish the shed while he is here, as it is nothing but trouble; and what about asking him to fit burglar bars, such as we had in Botswana? Maybe they are now appropriate here in Berringden Brow.

It is February 29th, Leap Year Day. At teatime, I come across Ben looking rather forlorn behind the counter in an almost deserted library.

"Where is everybody? "

Ben shrugs. "I don't know; it's been quiet all day."

"Oh well, perhaps they are all out proposing or being proposed to." I say lightly, browsing through the cinema and theatre leaflets on the counter.

"Please don't, as I'm single and would be obliged to accept," replies Ben, in his usual dry manner.

"Don't worry, I wasn't thinking of it." I laugh, picking up the leaflets for March.

If last year had been Leap Year I might perhaps have been tempted; but Ben is quite safe now. Anyway, he is only nominally single, being half of a co-habiting couple. The old custom of a bachelor having to accept a spinster's proposal on 29th February dates from well before these days of divorce being common and unmarried people living together. Anyway, I realised long ago that a bit of badinage across the library counter could hardly serve as the basis for a successful relationship, even supposing Ben had been unattached.

Changing the subject, I tell Ben that I have seen his paintings in the Art Club exhibition, whereupon he gloomily replies that nobody has bought them.

"Oh well, better not give up the day job just yet."

Chapter 36

I have to go to Leeds for a meeting about asylum seekers, as we have recently had a few turning up at the advice centre. I really hate going to Leeds, since I am invariably accosted by beggars. I do not mean the sort of beggar that sits and asks for change, and accepts it when you hurry by, I mean the roving kind, who pesters you and will not leave you alone. The Bristol beggars were always polite when I was working in that city, and I often gave them any available spare change, but the Leeds beggars are something else. Once, when attending an interview at the university, I arrived early and was sitting on the steps of the Parkinson Building, quietly eating my sandwiches, when a disreputable-looking man approached and asked if I could help him. I declined politely, and suggested he try Social Services, whereupon he replied that they would not help him, he was homeless, had nothing, and demanded that I buy him a cup of tea. I asked him, again politely, to please go away, but he just stood there, towering over me, intimidating me. There were about twenty people sitting on the steps at the time, but he had chosen me out of all of them to approach, and not one of them came to my assistance, ever when the man began swearing loudly at me. I became upset and threatened to call the university security, whereupon he finally left, with a parting salvo of 'f' words. Just what a candidate needs before a job interview…

The last time I visited Leeds I escaped relatively lightly, with just one request for twenty pence from a man wandering about in the precinct. He left me alone when I shook my head and went on to ask the next person, and the next, but with no luck.

On this occasion, I have to find the meeting venue in the Park Square area, and am walking briskly along Park Square East when a man some way off on the South side runs down the street, shouting and calling. I ignore him, hoping to reach my destination soon, but he catches up with me and snatches the papers with the details of the meeting out of my hand.

"You look like a very nice person..." he begins, in a strong Welsh accent.

"Appearances can be deceptive," I reply grimly, trying to retrieve my papers.

"You might be in a position to help me," the Welshman goes on. "You see, I need the train fare back to Merthyr, and perhaps a cup of tea before I leave."

I meanwhile, am frantically trying to remember the number of the building I need to be at, since my documents are evidently being held to ransom by this charmer from the valleys. I think it is number 47. The Welshman as if reading my thoughts, consults my papers. "You want to be at number 47; it's just up here on the left." He makes a show of opening the door for me and ushering me inside. The receptionist looks a bit startled, and I am afraid he will insist on being present at the meeting, as there are bound to be cups of tea available, but to my relief, he relinquishes my papers and retreats. I imagine the good people of Merthyr are not unduly sorry to be without him. But at least he did not swear at me. After the meeting, I dash back to the station, thankful to be part of the rush-hour crowds, head grimly down, hoping not to be singled out by any more dubious characters who think I look like a soft touch.

The next day, there is no sign of Jez, so I ring and leave a message. David calls back later to say that Jez has had to rush to Rotherham to fetch a ferret. As if I would be likely to fall for that old excuse…

Chapter 37

James Habergham has been asked to review a concert at Berringden Theatre featuring Evelyn Glennie in a performance 'Veni, Veni Emmanuel', and asks me to accompany him, promising that this time he will not forget the arrangement. Claire then rings and asks me to go with her. I tell her James and I will have free tickets in the circle, but that she is welcome to try to get a seat near us if there are any available. Claire says she does not want to make it a crowd of three and wonders if there is anyone else who would care to go. I remember that Jim the vicar likes this sort of music, so leave him a message. Jim rings back late saying he will make up the foursome. I then have the task of getting two extra seats; luckily, there are a couple left a few rows behind where James and I will be sitting, so these will have to do. As usual, I have arranged to meet James at the theatre, so Jim has offered to give me a lift, as he will be passing.

Jim comes to collect me in a BMW. Alex is impressed, and comments that vicars must be well-paid, but I do not imagine this is the case, as Jim has simply borrowed the car while his brother is overseas. I have told Claire to meet us in the bar, where I introduce everyone to everyone else, and note that James and Claire appear to take an immediate shine to one another. I give Claire and Jim their tickets; Claire is disappointed that she and Jim do not have such good seats as the ones James and I have been allocated, and I rather think she is hoping I will volunteer to swap with her. However, we are by now being asked to take our seats, so she has no option but to sit with Jim.

The concert is simply stunning, easily one of the most memorable evenings I have ever spent. Evelyn, dressed in attractive purple harem pants, dashes bare-footed from one percussion instrument to the next, giving a dazzling performance. Afterwards, James suggests a drink, but as Jim wants to go home, and since I am travelling in his car, I cannot accept. However, Claire immediately says she will be happy to accompany James, whereupon his eyes light up and they quickly disappear together into the bar. This leaves me with a star-struck vicar, who has apparently fallen in love with Evelyn Glennie and is already planning to take her sublime musical talent as the theme for his next sermon. Jim stops at a stall in the foyer to buy her latest CD, and after having dropped me off, rushes back to the vicarage, saying he wants to look at Evelyn Glennie's web-site. Everyone appears to have thoroughly enjoyed the evening for various reasons, not all of them connected with music.

I decide to borrow an Evelyn Glennie CD from the library, where I find Ben busy re-organising the video collection. I express doubts as to whether we subscribers will ever be able to find anything ever again, rather like when they re-organise the supermarket making it impossible to locate the Pot noodles. Ben tells me that the video boxes take up too much space; the new system will rely on cards. He wearily waves one at me, by way of example.

"Did I ever tell you I was once in a film, Ben?"

"No, but I expect you're about to," Ben sighs. He appears to be under a cloud, but I hope my little story will distract him from his troubles, at least for a few minutes. Unluckily for him, the library is quiet at the moment, so I go ahead.

"When I was about ten a BBC film crew came to Tiverton to make a short feature and asked my Mum's Dramatic Society to be extras. The title was "Dumnomia" – I think that was the Roman name for the Exeter area – and it was about a girl who runs away from London and turns up in Devon. She outrages the locals by falling in love with the Squire's son. Anyway, of course it all ends in tears. We extras had to appear in a number of scenes to do with the village fete - my younger brother was in the sack race, and my elder brother was in the cricket team, while I was supposed to be presiding over a jumble stall. Oh, and we all had to watch an awful lot of Morris Dancing. I remember the actress playing the runaway girl – it was Polly James, before she was in "The Liver Birds" - had to come to my stall and examine the jumble, while eating a cream bun. To show her contempt for the whole feudal set-up, she had to shove the half-eaten cream bun into a hat on the stall. Because things were not quite right – the light, the sound, the camera angle – she had to do several takes, and I remember thinking what a waste of cream buns it was…"

Ben shakes his head, looking as if he does not believe a word, but realising that it is best to humour me on these occasions. I notice the glimmer of a smile, and am encouraged to believe that my attempt to temporarily divert his attention away from his woes may perhaps be having some slight effect.

"And when was this film shown?"

"Actually, it wasn't. Various people from Tiverton wrote to the director, (Leo Aylwen, I think his name was), asking when "Dumnomia" was to be screened, but it probably ended up on the cutting-room floor. Or perhaps it was lost, but will reappear one day and be shown as a piece of archive footage about the feudal system which clung on in the depths of the West Country, while everyone else was enjoying the swinging sixties. Who knows, it might become a cult film and be transposed onto DVD – I suppose they can they do that, by the way? And you'll be renting it out from this very library..."

"Of course I will," says Ben. Despite my attempt to cheer him up, he still seems quite unhappy, and I wonder what is wrong; however this is not the time or place to ask, and he probably would not want to tell me anyway, so I gaze across the counter, and say the first thing that comes into my head.

"Wait while the clouds roll by, Ben."

He nods, then goes off to do some more shelving.

On Sunday morning, the congregation is somewhat bemused by Jim's sermon, which as I suspected, is a paeon of praise to Evelyn Glennie – her musicality, her style, her beauty, her accomplished performance, her personal triumph over deafness...

"You had a good evening, then, Vicar," comments one parishioner dryly.

Chapter 38

Nick astonishes me with an announcement that he is going to visit Pakistan. One of the Advice Centre clients is going to visit his family in Islamabad, and Nick has arranged to accompany him. They want to sort out an appeal for the man's son's wife, ho has been refused permission to come to the U K as her husband is disabled and the authorities think that he would be unable to support her. This means that I will

125

be in sole charge of the Advice Centre for two weeks, not an especially appealing prospect.

"I don't like being here alone, and it's not good practice either, anyone could wander in off the street and threaten me, or steal the petty cash; I just don't think it is safe for a woman to be here on her own."

"OK then, just keep the door locked and answer the phone."

Nick sends me an email from Islamabad to say that they have arrived safely and the appeal was successful. Now they are planning to have a few days holiday in Peshawar. At this, I gasp, since Peshawar, on the border with Afghanistan, Is a dangerous place for Westerners, in fact several have been taken hostage over recent years; I cannot think why Nick is going there. I email back expressing my horror, and he replies that the shoe-shine boy on the corner of the street where he is staying in Islamabad suggested they go there to visit his relatives, and I am not to worry as he will be going in disguise, dressed in shalwar kamise and a topi. I find this not in the slightest reassuring, it all sounds like something out of "Ripping Yarns". Nick always seems to get himself into some sort of scrape when overseas. Then I reflect that at least this particular adventure has the virtue of not involving any dubious women; it seems Nick will be fairly safe on that score in a Muslim country. Given the option of involvement with ruthless kidnapping bandits or ladies of the night, I'm not sure which is the better choice. Why can't he stick to Youth Hostelling?

My friend Hamish calls from Doncaster with a tale of woe concerning Louisa, his partner of twenty years. She has apparently fallen in love with a married Canadian man she has met via the internet, and is planning to see him later in the year. Meanwhile, she has told Hamish they can no longer sleep together, as she wants to be faithful to the Canadian. Hamish is understandably upset.

"I don't understand why she's doing this, Jess. One minute we were having al fresco sex on the canal bank, where her cries of 'Fuck me harder' were in danger of disturbing the local wildlife, and the next minute she says she loves this guy, and that we'll have to sleep with pillows down the middle of the bed. Is it the menopause, do you think? Have you been affected at all in that way?"

I am truly sorry for Hamish's distress, but assure him that, while I have indeed been affected by the menopause, I have experienced the more mundane symptoms, such as hot flushes, rather than a spectacular departure from sanity, such as Louisa appears to be currently exhibiting. I imagine most women would prefer a flesh and blood lover who took them onto the canal bank rather than a cyber lover who could come no nearer than an internet chat-room, although of course one can never be altogether certain about such personal matters. I am therefore quite prepared to stand corrected if someone publishes a survey using a representative sample of women of a certain age.

Chapter 39

Things begin to get rather difficult and confusing when Louisa calls, and starts twittering on about her new man, telling me how wonderful he is, how loving, accepting, generous, considerate. They are planning a romantic holiday in the Caribbean this autumn (Is it really wise to visit the Caribbean at that time – isn't it the hurricane season?) I venture to suggest that Hamish does not share her opinion of her cyber lover's wonderfulness, whereupon she tells me she 'has only one life'. But isn't this the allocation that most of us get? She then enumerates various matters which I must not on any account discuss with Hamish; oh dear, this is getting far too complicated. I'm not sure I can remember what I am and am not supposed to mention, and I don't think it is really fair to put me in this position. I say as much to Louisa, and she rings off.

Two weeks later, Nick is due back from Pakistan, but I am on tenterhooks in case he has been kidnapped. No ransom demand has so far been received at the Advice Centre, but that provides little reassurance. Eventually, Nick phones to say they have arrived safely at Manchester Airport and will be home in an hour. I almost weep with relief, but when Nick finally arrives, this turns to dismay. He is in a truly dreadful state, grey-faced and emaciated. He tells me that he has had an upset stomach for most of the time, and has become very dehydrated. The water was not safe, and there were no soft drinks available in the remote village beyond Peshawar on the north-west frontier where he has been staying. His friends were drinking river water and buffalo milk, but both these beverages made Nick extremely ill. He cannot tell me much more at the moment, as he is tired and has to keep running to the toilet, while I anxiously follow him round the house with a bottle of disinfectant.

"Do you want me to call the doctor?" I am really concerned at his appearance.

"No, I'll be all right." Typical man, feels awful but doesn't want to make a fuss.

"You look terrible. You'd better drink plenty of water."

I rummage in the medicine cupboard and find a packet or oral re-hydration salts, such as are used to give little children when they have tummy troubles. Goodness knows how many years it has been there. I mix up the contents of the sachet and give it to Nick, who is emerging from the bathroom once more, making a note to add toilet paper to tomorrow's shopping list.

It is more than a week before Nick starts to feel better, during which time he sticks to a liquid diet, and I have to do four extra loads of washing. Gradually, his colour returns and he looks less gaunt. Needless to say, he has not been to see his mother while in this sorry state since he does not want to worry her by tuning up looking as though he is at death's door. (Of course, he had no such scruples about visiting me.)

Meanwhile, Alex says he has a sore arm. At first, I imagine this is some ploy to avoid having to go to school, but when I examine Alex's red, swollen and twisted arm I realise that it might be broken.

"We'd better go to Casualty Alex, and get that looked at. What happened?"

"I dunnow, it just appeared."

I sigh, as of course, it cannot have just appeared, perhaps Alex has fallen and injured himself without realising it while under the influence of some mind-altering substance. We arrive at Casualty to be informed that there has been a serious accident on the motorway, and Alex will not be seen for some time. Of course, we realise that accidents have priority, so settle down to wait. The waiting room has been refurbished recently and is a lot more comfortable than it used to be when Alex was a regular visitor here as a toddler; he was always getting into some sort of trouble, swallowing my cough medicine (which was on a high shelf, but which of course I should have kept locked away), falling off his bike and breaking his arm, or getting scalded with a cup of coffee which Nick had left within reach and I was just about to move. I was always afraid he would be placed on the 'at risk' register, since he was so accident-prone, and that I would be characterised as an abusive parent rather than a harassed single mother of two lovely but lively sons. However, Social Services must have had more pressing matters to see to, as they never darkened our doors.

Alex settles into a chair and starts watching television, while I read my library book. Soon he is fast asleep, and I have read three chapters. Alex then wakes and asks for something to eat, so I go in search of sandwiches and tea. We eat our lunch watching Sky News, then do a magazine trivia quiz together, followed by the general knowledge crossword. The unfortunate accident victims have been trundled into the building by a separate entrance, and there are no heart-stopping sights to disturb us. It is a long time since Alex and I spent this length of time together, and this away-day to Casualty is proving quite relaxing. Alex then starts watching children's afternoon television and I return to my book. Eventually, at tea-time, Alex's name is called. The doctor says he must have an X-ray, so we have to join another queue. The arm is not broken, just very badly sprained. It is his right arm, and luckily he is left-handed, so has no excuse not to do his homework.

"Thanks for bringing me, Mum," says Alex as we return to the car.

"That's OK, all part of the service."

"It's a good thing I've still got a mother; Snuff lost his, and he's fucked."

"Language! I'm glad you sometimes appreciate me."

"I always appreciate you. It's just that, often I don't realise that I do."

"Well, it would be nice if you could try to realise it a little more often."

"I suppose so. I missed you when you threw me out, although it was good not to have you nagging me."

"I missed you when I threw you out, although it was good not to have you swearing at me."

"But all kids swear these days! It's part of teenage culture."

"And all mothers nag. They always have, and always will. It goes with the job."

Chapter 40

At the Advice Centre I check the weekly newsletter circulated by the Berringden Volunteer Bureau. In among the pleas for helpers with Community Transport, Sunday Care, Meals on Wheels and the Mental Health Befriending scheme, there is a request for someone to work for two weeks in Finland, helping to organise a conference on Women's Rural Development in the European Community. It seems that the conference will attract delegates from all over Europe, but is to be held in English, as the most commonly spoken EU language. There will be translators available, but the final report must be in good written English. I ask Nick if he can spare me for two weeks, and he says it will be fine, as the Easter holidays and the Muslim Eid festival are coming up, and the advice centre will be closed for several days in any case. We always notice a down-turn in the numbers of clients coming in before public and religious holidays, but they all come trooping back in droves on the morning the advice centre re-opens.

I email my cv, as requested, to Anna, the conference co-ordinator who is based in a town lying on the Arctic Circle, of which I have, unsurprisingly, never heard. I later receive a reply, with various documents attached. It seems that I have been appointed, and Anna would like me to start at once by editing the workshop programmes, which have been translated from Finnish into rather strange English. All the preparatory work can be done via email, and there is no need for me to go to Finland until just before the conference.

But what of Alex, surely I cannot leave him and the house to the mercies of his dubious friends? Amazingly, I will not have to, as Alex is going to a boot camp over the Easter holidays. Actually, that's not true – he is going on a sailing expedition around the Azores. Someone at Youth Club was meant to be going but had to drop out at short notice, and rather than waste the opportunity, Alex was asked to take his place. There is a bursary, so I will not have to pay anything. The instructions for the voyage state that there can be no drink, drugs or sex on board, and the crew members must be prepared to do all sorts of duties, including cleaning the toilets, something Alex has hitherto never been known to do; so it all does sound rather like a boot camp, but floating in mid-Atlantic.

I am amazed that Alex wants to go – this is the son who last year declined to accompany me on an hour-long pleasure cruise up the Exe estuary, which was at the time as calm as a mill-pond, on the grounds that he might be sea-sick. The boy who was distinctly green when sailing on Lake Kariba for a few days during our African sojourn, under the guidance of Captain Robin and his motley crew. The child who spent the entire ferry journey from Cyprus, where we were visiting friends in Limassol, to the Holy Land retching and throwing up in our hell-hole of a cabin, (one memorable New Year's Eve, long ago and in happier times, when people could visit Bethlehem and other West Bank towns without fear of being caught in the cross-fire). Going by these past experiences, Alex is no sailor, so I hope, both for his sake and that of his fellow crew members, that he manages to get his sea-legs pretty quickly on this voyage. We check web-sites of the Azores and Finland; the Azores appear to be quite stunning, with dramatic volcanic scenery and a variety of vegetation, while Finland seems to consist of lakes and trees. I remind Alex that I am a much better sailor than he is, but unsurprisingly, he does not want to swap.

I have never been to Finland, or indeed any of the Northlands, before. I have to change planes in Helsinki, and it is dark when I finally arrive at the airport of the university town on the Arctic Circle, having flown over numerous lakes and trees and seen a wonderful sunset. Anna is there to meet me. She drives me to a rather seedy-looking commercial hotel in the town centre where I am to be billeted, and leaves me with the programme for the following day. Apparently there is to be a meeting at nine o'clock in the conference centre attached to the swanky hotel where it seems everyone except me and the Estonian contingent, is billeted. Anna explains that I count as staff for the purposes of the conference, whereas the others are delegates, whose organisations are paying their expenses. The Estonians are not yet members of the EU, so they are staying in holiday cottages at a nearby lakeside resort.

The next morning I find the dining room full of commercial types who are visiting the town's paper mill, so I eat my breakfast alone and then set out to find the conference centre. Anna has provided me with a map, so finding the building is no problem, but when I get there I cannot find the way in, since all the doors appear to be locked. I shake and rattle them, but to no avail. There are no bells or entry-phones that I can see, and it is all extremely perplexing. Next, I walk all the way round the building, trying to work out how to gain entry. By now, it is coming on to rain, and I am on the point of giving up, when I notice someone looking out of an upstairs window. I call and wave, and the woman signals to me to go to the next-door hotel. Having consulted the receptionist, who luckily speaks perfect English, she kindly arranges for a porter to escort me downstairs to the basement, through a tunnel and up into the conference centre, where I emerge to find a group of people listening to Anna telling them something important in Finnish – evidently the meeting is well under way. I apologise for being late and explain that all the doors were locked, and I could not find the way in, feeling very foolish. Anna introduces me, and conducts the rest of the meeting in English for my benefit. I note that I am down to run one of the three workshops, with delegates from various EU countries, and of course, Estonia, so realise I should pay close attention to the arrangements.

After the meeting, Anna takes me to the offices of the organisation hosting the conference, (for which I currently count as an unpaid member of staff), which are located near the university campus. We go to the students' canteen for lunch. Back at the office, Anna gives me a pile of documents which she insists must be edited before I leave that day; there are so many that I am obliged to remain at the office until seven o'clock, long after everyone else has gone home at four. I let myself out onto the street, clutching my map of the town, and realise that my route back takes me past the town library. As I am in no rush to return to the cheerless establishment that is my hotel, I decide to see if the library has any books in English. The librarian shows me a shelf of English books, from which I select a translation of the Kalevala, the Finnish folk epic; reading this is to provide my entertainment for the evening.

Chapter 41

The following morning brings another pile of documents to be edited, not all of which are connected with the conference – I suspect Anna intends making full use of having me as an unpaid editor at her disposal. I am informed that tonight the delegates will start to arrive, and there is to be a welcoming sauna followed by a swim in the river, where the water temperature is three degrees Fahrenheit. I regretfully decline, pleading another engagement and pass a delightful few hours tucked away in a cosy corner of the library, with my copy of the Kalevala. I reach the part where Aino drowns, and am really pleased to be merely reading about a cold river rather than actually experiencing it.

The marvellous thing about mobile phones is that you can send and receive text messages. I get one from Alex telling me he is enjoying the trip, although he feels sick, and that there are whales and dolphins close to the ship. Since the highlights of my stay in Finland so far have been discovering how to get into the conference centre, locating the public library and successfully avoiding a dip in the freezing river, I decide to wait a while before replying.

Further fun is promised the following evening in the form of a dance. This is apparently to mark the end of the winter elk-hunting season, and is to be held in a sort of open-air palais in the forest beside a lake.

134

There will be a fleet of free buses to take us out from the town and bring us back. Anna is not going, but several other people from work will be there, and a charming young woman called Ulla says she will look after me. I am relieved to discover that there is an indoor dance hall as well as the open-air bit, as it is too early in the season for out-door dancing. Entry to the dance and welcoming refreshments are free, as the whole event has been organised by some local farmers' group. Ulla introduces me to an American lady, so we chat away in English until a man asks her to dance. Ulla is also dancing, in fact it seems I am almost the only wallflower. There are hundreds of people whirling round the floor, but no-one asks me to dance, not Anna's boss, whom I have met briefly at the office, and who I feel should be more welcoming towards a foreign visitor, nor even the man who appears to be working his way round to every woman in the room. I express my disappointment to Ulla, who explains that you have to stand in a certain place and look at the men in a certain way if you want to be asked to dance. I tell her that such ploys are not necessary at the Berringden Brow Barn dances, and anyway, the American lady has received lots of offers, even though she and I were standing in the same place, and I had not detected any special 'come hither' look upon her face. I decide that middle-aged English women simply are not Finnish farmers' cups of tea, and take a stroll outside by the lake until I start to feel chilly. Returning to the dance hall I find that Ulla has been looking for me. She has an extremely unprepossessing man in tow, whom she has apparently brow-beaten into agreeing to dance with me. The only problems are that he speaks no English, reeks of drink, and is a terrible dancer. I totter round with him, more or less holding him up, really, as he is very drunk, and try to escape as the dance ends, but he clings to my arm, and hold up two fingers, in what I hope is not a rude gesture.

"Two dances – it is the custom to have two dances with each partner," explains Ulla, passing by in the arms of the man who wants to dance with everybody except me. So there is no help for it, we must go round again. Afterwards I rush to the ladies loo. The buses are going back at midnight, but it is only ten o'clock. I find myself wishing I had a copy of the Kalevala handy.

Mercifully, at midnight, we climb aboard the buses and return through the forest and past the lakes, to town. I sit with Jenna, another of the women from the office, as Ulla is with another friend. I notice that my drunken dancing partner is on the same bus, sitting a few rows behind us. As Jenna and I alight from the bus, he makes a grab at me. I shriek in surprise rather than alarm, whereupon Jenna gives him a voluble piece of her mind and, taking my arm, walks me firmly round the corner to my hotel. We catch a glimpse of my admirer drunkenly mounting his bike and cycling off in the opposite direction.

I am all for calling Jenna a taxi home, but she declines, saying that she will be perfectly safe, as what has just happened to me is extremely unusual in this small town on the Arctic Circle. She disappears into the quiet streets, leaving me to reflect on the strangeness of the evening and to recall the number of times I have been mugged, which is three. The first time was one Tuesday afternoon in Tiverton, as I was making my way home after Brownies, about forty years ago. In those days Tiverton held a Tuesday Cattle market, and all the pubs stayed open throughout the day. As I walked through the town in my Brownie tunic, I felt a painful thwack on my head. Turning round, I saw that a ruddy-faced man, dressed in a brown overall and tweed cap, the habitual attire of a cattle drover, had hit me with his stick. He then went on and hit the next person, a pony-tailed young woman, over the head. She turned round, grimacing in pain. I was starting to weep, more with shock than pain. The man made his way along Fore Street, thwacking as he went – always females, I noticed, he must have thought we had escaped from his herd. By the time I reached the bottom of our hill, where my mother usually met me, I was in quite a state. I was nine yeas old and had never been mugged before. Dotey marched me straight round to the Police

Station, but the desk officer was unperturbed, almost implying that " if 'ee do let a little maid walk about in town of a Toosday then ee can expec problems …"

No-one else who had been hit by the drunken cattle drover complained, evidently they took the same sanguine attitude displayed by the desk officer, that anyone with the temerity to walk along Fore Street on cattle market day only has themselves to blame if things go wrong. After this, Dotey arranged for me to be escorted home after Brownies by a neighbour who worked in a town centre office. I only had to walk as far as the offices of Pearl Assurance and my escort would accompany me home, armed with her umbrella.

However, membership of the Brownies was turning out to be quite hazardous for me. Once a year, there was something called the Brownie Revels, which were usually held on the wettest Saturday in June, at the stately home of the local baronet. Of course, the Brownies were not admitted to the lovely house, the Revels were held in a hut in the woods, where the noise of a hundred little girls shrieking and screaming could not interfere with aristocratic living. This particular year, I had been called upon to construct a miniature garden for a competition, one of the more sedate branches of revelling, and had won a prize for my efforts, so was feeling very pleased with myself as I skipped home. Unfortunately, my route took me past some allotments, and at the end of the path leading to the allotments were three big boys, brandishing sticks. One of them accosted me.

"Get down that path!"

"No!" I turned round, trying to escape, but the other two lads were right behind me, grinning in a menacing, terrifying manner. They all started hitting me with their sticks – apparently the weapon of choice in nineteen-sixties Tiverton – but luckily for me, someone came by on the other side of the road, and the cowards disappeared down the path towards the allotments. I ran home as fast as my short legs and mounting hysteria would allow, to be met by Jack, my father, and Peter, my younger brother, on a search party sent out by my mother, who was by then worried that I was late returning from the Revels. After they had calmed me down, I explained what had happened, and we returned to the house, where Jack bundled Peter and me into his car. He drove us to the allotments, where the three lads, still armed with their sticks, were waiting on the path for their next potential victim.

"Those the boys?" Jack got out of the car and, with Peter and I peeping from the rear window, he decked the three, almost in one fell swoop, leaving them lying in a heap in the mud wondering what had hit them. My father was over six feet tall and powerfully built, and these days would no doubt be facing an assault charge. Times have changed, and nowadays no-one would dream of allowing their little girl to make her own way home from Brownies. The fear of 'stranger danger' is often said to be exaggerated, and parents are criticised for curtailing their children's independence; but having been assaulted twice in one year in a small Devonshire town, I am with the protective parents all the way. I myself would have appreciated a bit more mollycoddling. The streets were not safer then, we simply imagine that to have been the case. In reality, there always were men with sticks waiting to beat unwary little Brownies.

Chapter 42

The next time I was attacked was in Africa, the weapon this time being stones rather than sticks. I was walking in the early afternoon along the path leading back to Robin's school from the centre of Selebi Phikwe, a mining town in the north of Botswana. I did not usually walk about on my own, generally Alex was with me, but on this occasion he had gone to play with a friend who had a swimming pool in his garden. My attacker ran past me, which in itself was unusual, for Africans do not tend to run about in the mid-day heat. Then he turned to face me, and rushing back, he lunged for my shopping bag, which I instinctively clung on to. The thief managed to grab the handle, which came away from the bag, and fled off into the bush, but realising he had only the useless handle, he became nasty, and began throwing stones. I dropped the bag, containing my money, passport and travellers cheques, some of which I had been to the bank to cash. My screams alerted the security guards at Robin's school, and also reached Robin in his cottage, but help arrived too late. I was cut, bruised and very distressed, so Robin, who had no car, took me to a neighbour's house to ask for a lift to the Police Station. There was another friend there, who suggested we all immediately look for the passport.

"But there's acres of bush out there, it could be anywhere!"

The friend, Wesley, explained that it was likely that the passport would have been dropped on one of the paths. So without pausing even to wash my wounds, which luckily were only superficial, we set off across the river to the township. Almost immediately, we were approached by two tiny children.

"Lady's bag; lady's passport."

They took us along a side path where we found my shopping bag and the passport. Of course, my Travellers' cheques and money were missing, but the insurance would cover these items. At least I was spared the inconvenience of going to Gaborone, the capital city 200 miles away, to get a new passport. We thanked the children. By this time, there was a small crowd of Africans, all telling Wesley how sorry they were that this should have happened to a visitor to Botswana, and hoping that I would recover quickly. Dikeledi asked if she could take the bag to show the muti man, as he would look into it and be able to tell who it was who had attacked me; I let her have it, not so much for that reason, but because I did not want to use the bag again anyway, since it reminded me of an incident I was anxious to forget. So far as I am aware, the muti man never delivered a verdict in the case.

Emerging from this African reverie in northern Finland, I now have to face the conference. It goes well, with several people telling me how much they enjoyed my workshop, which is on barriers to women's rural entrepreneurship, and how these might be overcome. I have quite a large contingent from Italy, with a helpful young woman translating. The Estonians also require the services of an interpreter, but much to my relief everyone else speaks good English. I feed back to the plenary session, which is rather nerve-racking, as the other two work-shop leaders are a distinguished Estonian academic and a well-known Finnish journalist and writer on women's affairs. As merely a part-time voluntary sector advice worker from Berringden, I am somewhat overwhelmed to find myself in such illustrious company, but everyone is so kind and helpful to me and all goes well. The two other workshop leaders are presented with small gifts, but I am not, since I count as a temporary member of staff. One or two people comment on this, saying that all three workshop leaders should have been treated equally; there is further comment on the fact that I am a volunteer, staying in the run-down hotel rather than in five-star splendour. However, none of that really matters, the important thing is that people enjoyed my workshop and presentation, and found them informative and thought-provoking.

Anna tells me she will require the work-shop report written up before I leave, and that she will email the full conference report for me to edit as soon as she has received all the documents from the other participants. Meanwhile, we have more entertainment, this time at a restaurant housed in a Lapp-style circular tent. We all sit round the central fire and eat wild mushroom soup, smoked fish caught from the lake, and for afters, Lapp bread-cheese with cloudberries. Everything has been produced locally and tastes delicious.

Things get a bit raucous towards the end of the evening, as the Italians start singing risqué songs and one young woman gets the men standing up and beginning a strip-tease. Luckily, the fire is still burning brightly. The restaurant proprietor and his family start to look a little concerned, but when it is explained to them that people will not be removing their underwear, they relax and the proprietor even joins in. Next, the Estonians, not to be outdone, begin **their** party-pieces, and we all end the evening standing on the tables with arms linked, in what appears to be the Estonian equivalent of 'Auld Lang Syne.' I am the only English person in the room and cannot understand a word of what is gong on, but get the general picture. Everyone is so kind, and by the time we are ready to return to town I have received several invitations to visit Italy and Estonia, and many offers of accommodation if and when I return to Finland. Perhaps I'll come back one summer for the Kuhmo classical music festival, making sure to avoid all invitations to dances and river dips.

Chapter 43

I am glad to get home to see Alex, who has safely returned from the Azores, having fallen in love with a fellow crew member, Lorna, from Scotland, with whom he now spends hours each day on the phone. Nick has successfully held the fort, managing to look after the house and cat without mishap. His holiday photographs from Pakistan have come back, and he proudly shows me the pictures of him in his Asian disguise; luckily, he is dark and was able to remain inconspicuous amongst a crowd, provided of course that he did not open his mouth. The people he was travelling with had to explain that he was mute, if asked why he said nothing. Looking through the photos of the dramatic scenery on the north-west frontier, I come across a picture of Nick holding a Kalashnikov, not a typical holiday snap. I demand an explanation.

"Oh, the people in the village we stayed with told us not to use the front door as they have been feuding with the next-door neighbours for three years," says Nick nonchalantly.

"Why, was their honeysuckle growing over the fence?"

"And there were these guns everywhere. They insisted I had my picture taken holding one. They all know how to use them, and gunfire is quite common."

He removes the gun photo. "I don't think I'd better show that one to Mother."

I will soon have to start packing up for the move, and there is so much to be done. The Housing Association says it will be able to buy my house in June, and I have the little terraced house opposite a cricket field in Heptonroyd to go to. Frank comes with me to look at it, but I soon regret having brought him.

"Ugh, this house is so small! Nick warned me – he says he doesn't like it very much. And there's no garden, just a back yard and this tiny strip at the front. And you are overlooked at the back…Heavens, what's that noise?"

"It's someone mowing the grass on the cricket field. I suppose they have to do it a couple of times a week in the season. It's nothing dreadful. And the house we're in now is overlooked at the front, but we have this lovely view here. And anyway, I don't want a big garden – no-one helps me with it, it's just a chore, especially in the hay fever season, when gardening makes me ill."

I feel cross with myself for even trying to justify my choice of house to Frank, as it is nothing to do with him and anyway, he lives in a former coal-board house on a dismal estate, with a huge overgrown, untended wilderness of a back garden. I might have known that he would have nothing good to say about the house, since pessimism is his strong suit. As far as I am concerned, this house is in a good location, near the shops and railway station, and small houses are easy to heat and relatively inexpensive to maintain. Alex says he likes it, which is more important to me than Nick's opinion, as he can always return to his mother's if he wishes; and I like it, which is what really matters.

Robin has been allocated a council flat in Berringden town centre, in a tower block which houses retired people. There is a lunch club three times a week in the common room, organised by the residents, to which Robin invites me one Monday for meat and potato pie followed by fruit salad. Robin pays for me; it is £1.50 plus ten pence for a cup of tea, wonderful value for a satisfying meal.

"We know how to show a girl a good time," says Robin, placing my fruit salad before me with a flourish. I am not sure that the other, mostly rather staid, residents know quite what to make of him; he seems to be regarded as some sort of after- lunch cabaret as he goes round the room collecting up the cups.

Robin has no furniture to speak of, but I have found him a couple of chairs, some bedding, plus several items of crockery and cutlery, and other people in the flats are eagerly off-loading their unwanted effects. Robin will be fine.

Jez the rodent-fancying handyman finally arrives to fix the upstairs window-locks, all being quiet on the ferret front. I ask him to demolish the shed while he is here, so that the druggies have nowhere to skulk. Jez shakes his head.

"That's a big job, I'd need to disconnect the power cables, and have you thought about how you would dispose of all the rubble? Why go to all the trouble if you are moving anyway- let the new owners do it if they want to."

I have to agree that this makes sense, so the shed, scene of Alex's secret drinking parties, his bonging sessions, and also last year's rooftop protest, when he objected to Frank spending the night with me, gets a final reprieve.

Chapter 44

"Oh, some chap from Ireland phoned while you were away in Finland, " Nick tells me that evening. "He said you last saw each other over thirty years ago."

"Well, who was it? Didn't you get the name or number?"

"No, I told him you were away and he said he'd ring again."

Well, this is strange, as I am not aware that I know anyone in Ireland. Thirty years ago – perhaps someone from university? Then I realise that it may be connected with that school reunion; we gave our contact details to the organiser, but I did not know that he would make them generally available.
Well, whoever it is will ring again if he wants to. And then, I suddenly realise that it will be Gilbert Brown, my very first boyfriend, with whom I went for long cycle rides, who came with me to church youth club, and also when I was babysitting for Dramatic Society members - with their permission, of course. He was a keen naturalist and sometimes permitted me to accompany him creeping about in the woods on bird-watching sorties, which invariably ended with me stepping on a twig and startling the woodpecker or whatever we were supposed to be looking for, much to Gilbert's annoyance. He also took me canoeing on the River Exe, much to my mother's consternation, as she of course always imagined that I would drown. Gilbert had not been at the reunion, no-one mentioned him to me, and I have not least idea of him being in Ireland – in fact the last time I heard of him, he was working in Canada. But somehow, inexplicably, I know it is him who has telephoned while I was away.

Gilbert phones again on Sunday evening. Although he now has something of an Irish accent, I can still recognise his voice. We exchange news of our respective families – he is married, has three children and has pursued an academic career. I of course am not married, have two sons, an assortment of lodgers, and have had a strange medley of jobs, rather than a career. Gilbert seems rather disappointed at my reaction to his call.

"You're taking this very calmly," he complains. "I thought you'd be really pleased and surprised that I'd got in touch after all these years."

"Oh, it happens all the time, old school-friends getting in touch, reunions and so forth, now there are these special websites, " I tell him, airily.

Gilbert will not accept this. "But you were my first girlfriend – I was your first boyfriend. So **this** cannot have happened to you before. I thought you'd be really pleased to hear from me after all this time. Have you forgotten the canoeing, the bird-watching, the cycle rides – or the babysitting…?"

I still cannot work out quite why this man wants to claim a unique place in my affections, especially as he is happily married with a young family. And as for this grumbling at me, just because I am not squealing down the phone in delight …Gilbert is now suggesting that we meet up in the near future. He was unable to get across from Ireland for the school reunion, but is now asking me if I would like to visit. He owns a holiday cottage by the sea, where I could stay rent free; he would even collect me from the airport and bring me to the coast, if I could get a cheap flight. It all sounds quite tempting, and for an instant, I am almost persuaded to accept. Then I wonder whatever his wife and family would think of an old girlfriend turning up out of the blue, and realise that it would be quite inappropriate. Unless they have a different take on these things in Ireland. Gilbert is meanwhile enumerating the attractions of the area, the sea, the scenery, the wildlife – seals are common there apparently, the opportunities for canoeing, (I think I knew that canoeing would have to feature somewhere.) I thank him, but decline his invitation.

"Why won't you come?" (Goodness, does he really need it spelling out for him?)

"I'm afraid I've already made other plans for the summer."

"Oh." There is a pause, during which I rack my brains for some neutral topic.

"How is your sister? Is she still teaching in Devon?"

"Sarah – yes she's still there, with her family; she's a grandmother now. In fact, we're going over to see her soon. Jess! We could meet up in Devon. Didn't you say your brother still lives in Tiverton?"

"Well, yes, but as I say, I've made plans for this summer, I'm about to move house, and Jeff is also going away, I'm not quite sure when..."

Gilbert is determined not to let the matter rest. "Well, I've got your contact details, now let me give you mine. If you think you are going to be in the West Country this summer, then let me know." He reels off his home telephone number, mobile phone, postal and email addresses.

"I still think you are amazingly calm about this, Jess; I really thought you'd sound more pleased. It's almost as if you are trying to give me the brush-off. Didn't you ever think about me over the past thirty years?"

"Well; no..." That's not strictly true, as I did spot Gilbert in one of the old school photographs someone had brought to the reunion.

"I thought about you - a lot. And my first thought when I heard about the school reunion was to ask for your address. I had already made up my mind to try to find you. Something about being nearly fifty, I suppose."

"Actually, I'd rather not be reminded of that fact. And it was all a very long time ago, when we were very young... and we were never, well, you know, it was

146

very much a boy and girl relationship, wasn't it... " My voice trails off, as I really do not wish to say over the phone that Gilbert and I had never had sex. I simply do not see any need to get into that discussion after all this time. Nor do I want to remind him that it was him who finished with me, causing great hurt at the time to my inexperienced young heart, although I quickly got over it and consoled myself by joining a Youth Drama group and going out with Mick, another young thespian.

Gilbert's thoughts seem to echo mine. "Whatever happened to us, Jess?" he muses. I feel it is high time this conversation ended.

"Heavens, your phone bill will be astronomical! I had better let you go."

"All right; but don't lose touch, Jess; not now we've found each other again."
I put the phone down on one of the more extraordinary conversations I have had in my life, feeling quite cross because I have now missed "The Archers."

Chapter 45

Turning out some papers from a box in the loft, I come across some typed sheets, which turn out to be a collection of short stories I wrote some years ago. Of course, I have to stop and read them. Some are not too bad, but they all require polishing and putting onto the computer. Another job I do not really have time for at the moment, but maybe once we have moved... Then I realise that I must have thought about Gilbert at some point during the last thirty years, as one of the stories is based on our relationship as teenage sweethearts. In fact, many of these tales seem to have a similar theme of lost love. Funny, I can't even remember having written most of them. I had given the collection the title "Stories of Love and Misunderstanding." It is almost the story of my life.

The Gilbert Brown story, "First Love", is one of the better efforts. In it, he is called Patrick and I appear as Jane. They are sixteen, in the sixth form at school, and almost inseparable, although Jane's mother, who bears a strong resemblance to Dotey, disapproves of the relationship. Jane and Patrick go canoeing, cycling, babysitting and bird-watching together. Then Patrick develops an interest in classical music and starts spending more time with his neighbour, an older man named Clive, who has an extensive collection of gramophone records. Jane is sometimes invited to Clive's house to listen to the music, but always feels uncomfortable in Clive's presence; his behaviour to her is always polite but unwelcoming. Her suspicions that Clive does not really want her there are strengthened when her mother informs her that Clive has a reputation as a 'nancy-boy', one of the politically incorrect terms for gays in those days, when homosexual acts in private had only recently been decriminalised. Jane, not knowing what to believe, but upset to think that she is losing her boyfriend to the boy next door, tries to warn Patrick about what the town gossips are saying. Patrick takes little notice and increasingly seems to prefer his musical evenings to spending time with Jane. She then joins a youth drama group and gets over Patrick, as is often the case with first love. He appears surprised that she has switched her attentions from him, and tries to get her back by inviting her to go bird-watching with him, but Jane is now happily into drama, an activity generally carried out indoors rather than in dank woods or on draughty canal banks, and she has a new group of friends. Jane and Patrick then leave school and go their separate ways, to different universities.

So during all these years, had I thought about Gilbert at all, I would have imagined him to be gay. Now he has reappeared after thirty years as a family man in Ireland. Hence my prevarication over the phone - I could hardly say in response to Gilbert's enquiry as to whether I had ever thought about him, "Oh yes, I wrote a story about losing you to a gay man," when he now tells me he is married with three children.

Alex has a weekend job helping a friend and the friend's father do odd jobs, such as laying patios and putting up fences, so he gets up and goes out early on Saturday. I hear the door close behind him and snuggle down for another hour in bed. Then I think I hear the bathroom door close, but realise I must be imagining it, as there is no-one else in the house. It is quite a breezy morning, and the window is open, so the wind must have rattled the door.

Later, I go to town, locking the back door behind me. I am therefore dismayed to find, on my return, that the kitchen window is flying open and there is a distinct impression of a large training shoe on the work surface next to the sink, pointing towards the window. It appears that someone has been in the house, and since all the outer doors are locked, has been obliged to break **out** via the kitchen window. So far as I can see, nothing has been taken except a novelty African key-ring, without any keys. There is no evidence of any disturbance.

Naturally, I call the police. They agree that as there are no signs of anyone breaking in, the person must have already been in the house when I left and locked them in. I remember hearing the bathroom door close, and thinking that it was the wind. Now I realise that it must have been an intruder, who saw Alex go out early, and sneaked in the back door to use the toilet. The person must then have lain low in the house – presumably in Alex's room, until I left.
The only means of escape was to unlock the kitchen window and jump out.

This is all extremely strange and unnerving. The police think that whoever it was must have had knowledge of the lay-out of the house, as he was able to locate the bathroom and Alex's room without disturbing me. Possibly it was someone hiding out in the shed, and watching our comings and goings .I have given up trying to secure the shed door, since the locks are broken as fast I replace them.

I ask Alex if any of his friends has been hanging around; at first, he hotly denies that it could possibly have been anyone he knows, but then concedes that Snuff has recently been thrown out of his accommodation and is currently homeless. Perhaps it could have been him. Alex goes to look for Snuff, but there is no sign of him, and other lads report that he has gone to Leeds.

When Nick arrives home much later, having spent the day at Doncaster races, he discovers a large amount of money missing from one of his carrier bags. I am horrified, as I had no idea that Nick was keeping money in the house. How foolish, since he knows Alex is always bringing in waifs and strays. I am very upset at the loss of the money, and also at the thought of lying in bed while Snuff, or whoever, was hiding in the next room. Thank goodness we are moving very soon.

Just before we move, Alex remembers that Molly the dog's family will not have our new address, and urges me to ring and give them our new contact details. I add this chore to the list of things to do before Friday. When I eventually get round to it, I receive an unexpected response.

"Thanks heavens you've rung! Molly had pups ten days ago and we lost you phone number. We've looked, but you don't seem to be in the book."

"Goodness, what did she have? How is Molly? And how are the pups? And is the father dog a Staffie as well?"

"She had five boys and a girl. They're all doing well - she's a good mother. And the father is also a Staff, although they haven't got pedigree papers."

Straightaway I say that we would like to have the girl. I relay this exciting news to Alex, who wants to visit the canine family immediately.

"The pups will have their eyes open soon, let's wait until then."

"How soon can we get her?"

"We have to wait eight weeks, until the pups are weaned."

"It's hard to wait 'til then! Mum, we'll have to get a bed for her, and a nice collar and lead. And puppy food." It has been such a long time since I saw Alex so enthusiastic about anything.

"Yes, and she'll need her injections. Perhaps we can get a book about dogs from the library. There must be lots of things we don't know. And she'll have to go to obedience classes, I've heard that Staffies can be quite a handful. I'll find out where the nearest dog club is. What are you going to call her?"

Alex thinks for a moment. "Mash."

"Mash? That's a strange name. Why not Millie, seeing her mother is Molly."

"No, Mash, not Millie! My friend Tez had two dogs called Bangers and Mash.

Alex returns to his room, loudly and happily singing an improvised song about a bitch called Mash, while I wonder just what we are letting ourselves in for.

Chapter 46

As moves go, I suppose ours is relatively trouble-free. Frank, Nick and Alex all work hard helping the removal men, while my main tasks are to keep Nutty the cat shut in her basket and also not to lose track of the kettle or the radio, so that we can at least have a cup of tea and listen to ' The Archers' once we arrive at our new house. There is a spare attic room where the boxes can be stored unopened until I have the strength to deal with them, which may not be terribly soon. Finally, the removal men leave, and we all collapse round the kitchen table over a takeaway, while a disgruntled Nutty retreats to the wash-house, to lick her buttered paws.

Next day, I go into Berringden to notify the bank, council office and the library of my new address. Ben is not in evidence, and the counter staff report that he has gone home sick. I suddenly realise that today is his birthday; in fact, it is his fortieth birthday. (Ben did once tell me he was the same age as Eddie Izzard, but that was not true, as Ben is actually older.) No wonder he has gone home. I remember feeling quite miserable on my fortieth birthday, and wanting to quietly hide somewhere, only to discover that some friends had kindly arranged a surprise Sunday lunch party for three families including seven kids, so quiet was hardly the word. Of course, I quickly recovered my usual good spirits. Maybe Ben will soon be happier now that he has finally attained the age of forty, where life begins etc. etc. I do hope so.

Leaving the library, I spot a familiar figure in the precinct, it is Robin, carrying two shopping bags and dutifully following a lady into a discount chemists shop. Naturally, I go after him to say hello. The lady is looking at a shelf of hair care products, while Robin gazes about the shop with a slightly lost air.

"Hello, Robin; who's your friend?" Robin jumps.

"Oh, Jess; oh, I don't know – someone I've just met in the street. We got talking about these nuisances who chase you to ask for money for charity."

I try not to laugh, as this is obviously untrue. Robin is clearly on a shopping trip with this lady. She meanwhile has returned from perusing the shelves and has taken her place beside Robin, while we hastily finish our conversation; he is telling me about some guided walks which are on this week. I smile at her and introduce myself, as I know Robin will never do it. She does not smile, but tells me her name is Agnes. She then turns to Robin and announces that they are going for coffee; clearly I am not to be included in the invitation. Robin meekly follows her out of the shop and round the corner in the direction of Woolworth's. She certainly seems to have him well trained. I can imagine the conversation they might be having in the café, something along the lines of

"Who was that woman?" "I don't know, just someone I met in the street…"

Alex and I go to visit Molly, Mash and her brothers. They are extremely cute, but of course, little Mash is the cutest of them all. She is dark brown with a white chest and a pretty face, while the male pups are lighter in colour and less attractive. With her being the only bitch in the litter, Mike her owner says he could have sold her twenty times over, as people like to make money by breeding from them. However, mindful of the fact that he would not have got Molly back unless I had persevered valiantly over two days to find her rightful owner, Mike says he will let us have Mash for a much reduced price of £50, which I pay somewhat unwillingly, half- wishing we had kept Molly, since she had come free and was already house-trained.

In the library, I am searching for a book about Staffordshire Bull Terriers when I notice Robin, apparently alone, checking the internet. I enquire after Agnes, commenting that she looks as though she is the sensible sort of woman who cooks the good roast dinners Robin loves. "You've guessed it, old bird. "

"And how does **she** react when you call her 'old bird'?"

"Ah, old bird, I wouldn't dare call her 'old bird', as she might take offence…"

Mash the puppy duly arrives at eight weeks old and proceeds to chew everything in sight. The boys once had a story-book about a monster named Crammus, who ate everything including the school, and I feel that Mash must be related, and the book's author must have derived inspiration from watching the antics of a Staffordshire Bull Terrier. The kitchen chairs, the cupboards, her basket, are all gnawed at, and one teatime Nick and I watch in horrified amazement as she swiftly devours a plastic strip from the bottom of the washing machine. Alex foolishly takes off her collar and gives it to her to play with, and of course she eats that as well. It is not that she has no toys – we have lavished playthings upon her - balls, bells, plastic sausages, squeaky rubber bones, the best the pet-shop can offer. Mash seems determined to ignore our gifts and to eat her surroundings instead. Naturally, there are lots of odd spills to mop up, and we seem to spend weeks with the kitchen floor strewn with soggy newspapers, but on the whole we are glad to have her. She seems to have as charming a temperament as her mother, Molly. And taking her for walks is definitely doing me good, as not only am I getting regular exercise, but I am also getting to know all the neighbours, who stop to admire pretty little Mash and chat to me.

I would recommend getting a dog to anyone who was lonely, as dog owners seem to be a very friendly bunch of people, so you quickly have human, as well as canine, acquaintances.

Chapter 47

During the next few weeks I begin to discover the pros and cons of living in Heptonroyd. One of the advantages is the Community Centre, where all manner of groups meet. I find there is to be a belly dancing 'taster' class next week, for women only, run by a lady named Candy, who has trained in Cairo. I inform Alex that I am off to a belly dancing class, whereupon he predictably sniggers, but I tell him that it is well known that such dancing is good exercise.

"Yeah, right, Mum, if you say so," is his amused response. About seventy women have gathered, and there is also one man, but he turns out to be the photographer from the local paper, who takes his pictures and then beats a hasty retreat. We are taught to shimmy, wiggle and step by an extremely accomplished lady of generous proportions, and I suddenly find myself wishing that I lived in those lands where slimness is not so prized as it is here.

Candy has brought an array of her elaborately decorated costumes for us to inspect; and they are very definitely not of the seven veils variety, since Egypt, where Candy goes to hone her skills, is a Muslim country and not even bare midriffs are permitted. The tops and bottoms of the belly-dancers' outfits must be joined by nets with clearly visible seams.

I recall that Nick and I and the boys once stayed in a village pub that did Bed and Breakfast, in the depths of Gloucestershire. The boys were watching television in their room, having had their tea at a burger café, and Nick and I were eating a pub supper, when the usual pub background musak abruptly stopped, only to be replaced by exotic Eastern music. Two young belly dancers then entered unannounced, and began shimmying round the lounge bar. Most of the customers, apparently local regulars, took not the slightest bit of notice and carried on playing dominoes and cribbage. After a bravura ten -minute performance, the girls sashayed out, the Arabic music was turned off, and the musak resumed. Nick and I looked at each other, open-mouthed in astonishment but nobody else reacted in any shape or form.

I enjoy the evening, but do not imagine that I will enrol for a course, as I have found the whole thing quite exhausting. Cricket appears to be less strenuous, and I enjoy watching the games on the field opposite my house, until one day someone hits a six, which smashes my bedroom window, and I discover the disadvantages of my new home's location The players are quite unconcerned, simply producing another ball and carrying on with the game, but I feel fairly aggrieved and run onto the pitch in an effort to attract the captain's attention.

"That's my window you've broken!" He is in the middle of a run and does not appreciate my intervention.

"Get off the pitch!"

"But I want to know what's going to happen about my window!"

"Go and see that man over there who's scoring." I approach the scorer.

"Ring this number – 0142…."

"Hold on, I need a pen." I snatch the scorer's pen, whereupon he protests that he needs it to write down the scores, adding that I am not the first person to have a window broken.

"Well, maybe, but it is the first time I have had a window broken." Of course I have no paper, and resisting the temptation to tear a page from the sacred cricket score book, I write the telephone number on my arm, thinking they could have called a halt for five minutes to deal with my query as to who will pay for the broken window; it would certainly have been more courteous than playing on regardless. As I am leaving to go to inspect the damage, some wag asks if they can please have their ball back, since they cost £15.

My bedroom is in a dreadful state, there is glass everywhere, on the bed, carpet, chair, amongst my clothes, in the bedding, over the desk and the computer. It takes me two hours to clear up. At first, there is no sign of the ball but then Mash finds it under the bed, and spends a contented hour chewing it. She emerges covered in crimson, which I immediately imagine must be blood from a glass injury, but to my relief, it turns out simply to be dye from the ball. I call a glazier who says he can come tomorrow. Lucky it is not winter. .
The following day, the glazier's boss rings to tell me that his worker has rung in sick, and it will be the day after before they can come and fix the window. Meanwhile, I am still finding glass fragments in the flower-pots by the front door and on the window ledge. Oh well, I suppose this is the risk run by anyone buying a house with delightful uninterrupted views over a cricket field. One of the neighbours tells

me his windows have been smashed twice. I imagine the cricket club's insurance premiums must be quite steep.

The glazier appears on Tuesday, and I call the club chairman to come and pay him, as of course I have insufficient money. He asks for the return of the cricket ball, but when I produce the chewed specimen his face falls.

"We can't even practice with this! We might have to charge you for it."

"By all means, send the bill to the dog and she'll pay you in doggie chews."

Needless to say, I hear no more on the subject.

Chapter 48

"Mum, I think this house is haunted!"

I am beginning to think that Alex is right, as there have been a number of strange, unexplained occurrences since we moved in. The mirrored sliding doors of the bathroom cabinet crashed into the sink - how did that happen? Lights in the front room and the hall mysteriously switch themselves on and off, in a very disconcerting manner. At first, I put this down to a fault in the electrical wiring. Now, and this is the most worrying thing of all, something is trying to ignite the gas taps on the kitchen stove. Sitting in the front room, I hear the clicking noise of the starter switch, but when I go to the kitchen, the switch is clicking way eerily by itself. Luckily, the gas itself has not been switched on, but I am extremely frightened and call Alex down from the attic.

"Alex. Come and look at this!"

"Perhaps someone died here recently. We'd better get the house exercised."

"Exorcised. Yes, I'll ring the vicar."

Jim takes the matter seriously, and says he will come round and pray, which I really appreciate. And thankfully, the power of prayer really works, as the troubled spirit stops playing with the mirrors, lights and gas taps and goes away. People can be sceptical or scornful about these matters, but there has actually been research done which shows that people who have prayers said for them tend to recover from illness better than those who do not. This happens even when they do not know that they are being prayed for, so the results cannot be put down to any psychological effect.

Lorna, Alex's Scottish girlfriend, is staying for a week. She seems a nice girl, but she is very quiet, and when she does speak it is with an extremely broad Scots accent, rather as if she could be related to the television character Rab C Nesbitt, so that I have considerable difficulty understanding what she is saying. Still, she and Alex seem happy together, although I cannot help wondering whether Lorna is not getting rather fed up with going out drinking with Alex's mates every night. I ask her what she likes to do when she is at home, what interests and hobbies she has, and she replies that she enjoys going to the cinema. We discuss the controversial Ken Loach film, "Sweet Sixteen", which was set near to where she lives. Always anxious to help my guests enjoy their stay, I contrive to get Alex on his own.

"Alex, why don't you take Lorna to the pictures one night instead of out with your friends? I'm sure she would enjoy the change."

"The pictures? No way! Why, have you been talking to her?"

"Yes, as a matter of fact it did come up in the conversation."

"Well, she's never mentioned it to me."

"Maybe **you** should ask her. She's your girlfriend, not another of the lads, and girls enjoy doing different things."

"Such as?"

"Well, girls like gong out with a boyfriend as a couple rather than being with a gang of friends all the time."

"I'll take her if you'll let me have the money."

"Alex, she's **your** girlfriend! Besides, I don't have much spare money, what with an extra mouth to feed this week."

"Why do you **never** have any money?" asks Alex. "Did you **ever** have any?"

"Well, I did once manage to save up a couple of thousand pounds, but I had to let Tom have it to pay off his student overdraft, it was interest-free as long as he was a student, but of course interest is added on now he has graduated. It's better that he owes me the money rather than lining the pockets of the bank's shareholders. And he is repaying me every month."

"So, do you think you **will** ever have any money?" persists Alex.

" No, I don't suppose I ever shall, certainly not on the wages I earn now."

"Why don't you try doing the lottery?"

"Because there's probably more chance of catching the ebola virus!"

"Someone's got to win it…"

"Yes, and someone's got to catch ebola."

"Well, I'll be OK, 'because I shall inherit this house," says Alex, complacently.

I tell him not to be too sure, as I might leave it to the dog. She's less trouble.

Next morning, Alex presents me with a list of videos he would like me to bring from the library, if they are available, for him and Laura to watch. It is not until I am handing the list to Ben that I realise they that all have a common theme.

"Hmm; 'Train-spotting', 'Fear and Loathing in Las Vegas', '200 Motels'... Quite a selection. Whatever happened to rom-com, Jess? I think you'll find that these are all drug-related movies..."

I suppose I might have guessed.

Chapter 49

A message appears on my answer-phone. "Jess, it's John Peters in Exeter. Auntie Phyl is sinking fast, you should come quickly if you want to see her."

My dear godmother is over ninety, so this news is not totally unexpected, but it is sad to think that her life is ending. Auntie Phyl has been so good to me since my own mother died thirty years ago, I call Exeter Youth Hostel and book in for tomorrow, as my brother is away for the summer and his house is shut up, so I cannot stay there. Looking at the calendar, I suddenly realise that this is the week that Gilbert Brown and family will be in the West Country, visiting his sister. Maybe I should get in touch with him after all. I do have his mobile phone number. I'm still not sure about it, but what if I said nothing and then ran into him? That would be embarrassing. I suppose meeting for a coffee and chat would be OK, just as long as he did not want to take me canoeing or bird-watching; surely his wife would never allow that, I would be quite safe. I dial his number, and we arrange to meet at the Canal Tea Gardens, close to where I used to live, at eleven o'clock, in two days time.

I spend the next day on the motorways, driving three hundred miles south in my reluctant, borrowed vehicle, which normally goes no further than Asda. Arriving in Exeter, I phone John, my godmother's nephew, to arrange a visit. John and his wife Mary have kept an eye on Auntie Phyl ever since she lost her husband, Uncle Cecil, a few years ago. My godmother's house is at the top of a steep hill overlooking the city. She and Cecil had been of the opinion that there was going to be a great flood, of Old Testament proportions, and that hilltops would be the only safe places. They had been very relieved when I told them that Berringden Brow was a hilly area, as previously I had lived in the flat lands near Selby, obviously ripe for inundation when the worst happens. I think that they were ahead of their time, regarded as eccentrics; but with all this global warming who's to say that they will not indeed be proved right in the end? I coax my car up the one in four gradient, not without some difficulty, as I am down to first gear and the engine is boiling up. Mary meets me at the door of the house, explaining that I must prepare myself.

"She's so altered from when you last saw her, Jess. Try not to be too upset."
Mary leads me into the front room, where there is a huge hospital bed containing a small Auntie Phyl. She appears shrunken and grey, somehow. I can scarcely recognise her. Then I realise that for the first time in my life, I am seeing my godmother without her hair being done.

"Jess is here," says Mary. I take Auntie Phyl's hand and quietly hold it.

"Jess," Auntie Phyl breathes, before sinking back into a doze.

"She's asleep nearly all the time now," explains Mary. "The end is very close."

I watch the small sleeping figure for a few minutes, then can bear it no longer.

I gently kiss her goodbye, and leave the room. Mary follows me into the hall.

"How long are you staying in Exeter?"

"How long will it be?"

"The doctor thinks it will be only a matter of days."

"I'll stay."

What I mean of course is that I will stay until after the funeral, but it seems indelicate to mention this with Auntie Phyl still alive. I give Mary my mobile phone number, and make my way sadly back down the hill.

Chapter 50

The following day sees my appointment with Gilbert. I arrive at the Canal Tea gardens and sit trying to read a book. Gilbert comes at eleven o'clock, without his family, whom, he explains, have gone swimming at the Leisure Centre.

"This is just like old times," he begins, as I pour him a cup of tea.

"Oh really? I can't remember us ever having come here together. In fact, I don't think this place was dong teas when we lived here. Wasn't there an elderly couple in the cottage?" I am happy keeping the conversation general, but Gilbert smiles and, dispensing with preliminary chit-chat, weighs in with, "How did we begin Jess? I would never have had the courage to ask you out, you **were** so very pretty."

I'm not sure it is necessary for him to stress the ' were' quite so heavily.

"You were new in the sixth form, and I was secretary of the church Youth Club. I told you about the Friday evening meetings and you came along."

"Oh, so you were simply doing your secretarial duty, it wasn't that you liked me especially. I hoped that it was, and couldn't believe my luck. So I've been labouring under a delusion all these years."

"Evidently."

"And I walked you home after Youth Club."

"Yes, you did –but just that once. After that, you said that the hill where I lived was too steep, and you used to leave me at the round-about at the bottom."

"Surely not!"

"It's true! I had to walk up that long dark hill on my own. It was really creepy, especially passing the canal basin. I remember my mother took a dim view, she said that a boy should always see his girl-friend safely home."

"Well, I apologise for my lack of chivalry, thirty years ago."

"That's all right, it's all long since forgiven, if not forgotten."

In fact, come to think of it, Gilbert's actions set the pattern for the way most men have treated me over the intervening years. They have been 'leaving me at the roundabout' so to speak, ever since. I never liked walking home on my own, but was prepared to do it, or else I would never have gone anywhere.
By this time, we have finished our tea, and Gilbert suggests a walk.

"Isn't that copse where we went to look at the Lesser Spotted Woodpecker just along here?" he asks.

"Oh, is it? I'm not really dressed for scrambling about in the woods," I demur, although of course, I am dressed in my usual down-beat style.

"All right, we won't go into the woods, but I want to tell you something, and it won't do here," says Gilbert. This has the effect of making me want to remain in the Tea Gardens until dusk, but I realise that there is no chance of that as Gilbert grabs my arm and leads me along the towpath. We walk in silence, past the house where I used to live, past the bungalow where we used to baby-sit, until we arrive opposite the Lesser Spotted woodpecker copse, where we sit on a bench. I wonder what is coming next, and try to release my arm, explaining that I the pollen count is high and I need to blow my nose.

"Jess, did you really never think of me in all those years?"

"I did think of you occasionally. I fact I found this." Against my better judgement, I produce a copy of the 'First Love' story from my bag and hand Gilbert. He reads it silently.

"Jess, you were right about quite a lot of it. The Clive character did show me some strange photos and stuff like that. I told him I wasn't interested and stopped visiting him. Then I went to look for you again, but you were always doing drama classes and hanging out with Mick. Then, just before we were both going away to university, I saw you out in the town, shopping with your mother. Do you remember?"

I tell him, quite truthfully, that I have no recollection of this incident.

"Your mother never thought much of me, did she? You smiled at me, but she glared, and we just said hello and passed by. But I wanted so much to tell you, that I realised then that I did love you. And I have wished so often since that I had had the courage to tell you. But I was a coward, and I let you go away. And that's why I wanted to see you again, to tell you now what I should have said thirty years ago."

It seems like hours before I can find the strength to reply. I am sitting on a bench by the sunny canal,

164

surrounded by wild flowers, dragonflies, butterflies and bees, with the breeze playing in my hair and it is almost like being in a Mills and Boon novel, except that my noses is running, my eyes are itching, and there is an annoying tickle in my throat. So finally, in middle age, I get a man declaring his love for me – but thirty years too late.

"I really wanted to tell you," repeats Gilbert. I struggle with suppressed emotion and the effects of hay fever until I eventually find my voice.

"But you didn't take any account of whether or not I would want to hear it!"

Did he imagine that it would be some sort of consolation prize? Never mind that I've been a struggling single parent for years, the idea that someone miles away, married, with kids, whereabouts unknown for decades, actually loved me thirty years ago will suddenly make everything in my life better…is that what he thought? And if he **had** had the courage to speak, if he **had** managed to withstand my mother's disapproving look, how different our lives might have been – whatever good is knowing that to me now? It's just - irrelevant.

Gilbert looks genuinely astonished. "I certainly didn't intend to upset you."

"Well maybe men see things differently. Or maybe it's just me making too much fuss…"

My voice trails away, and I sneeze violently seven times. Blowing my nose, I suddenly leap up from the bench and hastily retrace my steps, telling the startled Gilbert that I must go back and try to find some fresh tissues.

"Can we please talk about something else? Atishoo! The usual sort of school reunion stuff - like the time the boys' tent blew down on the geography field–trip and you all had to move in with the girls? Atishoo!"

"Yes, but I was sharing the small tent with Gibby Marsden and Mr. Allen, so I missed all the fun."

"Oh, and I was in with Janice Pirbright and Miss Wooller who was meant to be chaperoning the girls. So I missed out on all the Atishoo! excitement as well."

"What about when you caught me and Andrew with a risque book, "In Praise of Older Women", as I remember, just as Andrew's parents came back, I think you were delivering the parish magazine, and neither Andrew or I wanted to be seen with it, we were passing it to and fro between us, and it dropped on the floor, so you picked it up and hid it in your pile of parish magazines?"

"Or what about the time we went canoeing at the Salmon Ponds and got really drenched..."

"Wasn't that when your knickers got wet and you took them off and hung them on a bush to dry but forgot about them and went home without them..."

"Atishoo! Oh, yes; maybe we'd better **not** talk about that then..." we laugh, at least, I sneeze and laugh, which results in a sort of agonised splutter, after which I start to feel a little better. When we reach the car park, Gilbert suggests that I get into his car for a moment. I hesitate, still sneezing.

"There's a box of tissues right here on the dashboard." Such seductive words.

I sit in the passenger seat, joyfully wiping my nose, as Gilbert puts a tape into the car audio system, and the strains of an old Kinks record ring out.

Gilbert looks at me knowingly. I look at him, puzzled, over the box of tissues.

"Don't you remember me playing you this? You used to like it."

166

"I still do like it, but no, I honestly don't recall you ever playing it for me."

Gilbert looks disappointed. "I brought it specially to play it for you again."

"Thank you for the days, those endless days, those sacred days you gave me.
I'm thinking of the days – I won't forget a single day, believe me.
I bless the light; I bless the light that lights on you, believe me.
And though you're gone, you're with me every single day, believe me..."

If I was trying to write some sort of romantic novel based upon my life, even I would draw the line at this. I simply couldn't make it up; yet it really is happening. However, by this time, I have had quite as much emotional turmoil as a middle-aged woman can take for one morning, so ask Gilbert to switch the tape off and put Radio 4 on, finding the measured tones of Brian Perkins reading the lunchtime news extremely comforting. Gilbert then remembers he has to go and collect his family from the Leisure Centre.

"I'll come with you, if I may - I'd like to meet them."

And so I am introduced to Sinead and the three children, in fact we all have lunch together at a burger bar, as the children are hungry after their swim, and that's what they want to eat, and I tell them about the time I visited Ireland with my sons, and Gilbert and Sinead exclaim and say that I must have unknowingly passed within yards of their family home when I took the Enneskillen road. And if they had known, we could have stayed at their sea-side cottage, instead of in the 'Brendan Behan' dormitory of the local hostel, where, as I had feared on learning its name, all the drunks were billeted. And it all goes well. Naturally we do not talk about canoeing or baby-sitting or bird-watching or Clive's music and pornography evenings, but keep the conversation general. Sinead is really nice, and so are the kids, and I am very pleased to have met them.

After lunch, I cheerfully wave them off in the direction of Gilbert's sister's house, and return to Exeter, where the Youth Hostel is full of excited French school children and I am therefore not obliged to talk to anyone, which is just as well, as I don't think I could. I just want to be left alone to ponder, not about what might have been, but what actually has been. And after thinking about Tom and Alex and my life as their mother, I reflect that really I would not change a thing, except for Alex's drug taking of course. If Gilbert and I had married, we would not necessarily have stayed together, since first love is not always true love, and people who marry their childhood sweet-hearts often find that their spouses change, develop new interests and opinions, become different people as they mature. Gilbert and I still had a lot of growing up to do when we were seventeen. I never have been one of those people who declare that 'things always happen for a reason', or believe that they always 'turn out for the best'; but in this case, I believe that they have. I find myself relieved that Gilbert was discouraged by Dotey's intimidating glare, and that we went our separate ways. I am far from being the sweet seventeen year old who left her knickers drying in a bush and went home without them.

It is odd that Gilbert appears to remember mostly good things about me, while it is the annoying things about him, such as the leaving me at the roundabout instead of walking me home, which appear to have stuck in my memory. He seems to have become more romantic over the years, (fancy bringing that Kinks tape for me to hear!), while I have become more down-to- earth. All in all, I am relieved that our meeting is now over.

Apparently, a number of marriages have broken up following school reunions, as people run off with former flames, but it certainly isn't anything I would care to do. I wonder what they find to talk about once they have exhausted the old school stories and

168

reminiscences. Can those who had teenage crushes or were first loves at school many years ago successfully relate to each other as mature adults? Perhaps someone should write a PhD about it– maybe I should submit a research proposal on the subject and go round interviewing people, the runners-away and those they have forsaken. But on reflection, it would probably be wiser to leave this topic to someone else.

I am not surprised when the phone rings later that evening, and John tells me that Auntie Phyl has passed peacefully away. The funeral will be on Thursday, at the small chapel in the crematorium. John explains that when you get to ninety, most of your friends have died, so not many people are expected to attend, and anyway, Auntie would not have wanted any fuss.

Chapter 51

Auntie Phyl's funeral is a quiet, dignified affair, led by a representative of the White Eagle Lodge. Auntie Phyl's two children pre-deceased her – one of the draw-backs of living into one's nineties - and she had no grandchildren, so John is the only close relative. After the service, everyone goes to John and Mary's house for lunch, and Mary gives me a photograph of Auntie Phyl, taken on her ninetieth birthday, which she has come across during the clearing up. It shows a gracious, smiling lady with an elegant hair-do, holding a lovely bouquet, which is exactly how I want to remember her. Mary also presents me with a plastic bucket containing seventeen packets of brown rice, discovered in Auntie Phyl's larder. Evidently this constituted part of the flood defences, since rice in this sort of quantity would have been a valuable food reserve had she and Uncle become marooned on their hilltop, sustaining them until the waters receded; or alternatively, it could have been used to fill sandbags. Mary explains that she and John do not care for brown rice, and asks me to take it all away. The packets are so old that they do not have sell-by or use-by dates, evidently pre-dating this consumer innovation. There appears to be sufficient rice to relieve famine in a small third-world country, so that I do not feel inclined to throw it away, although I doubt I will live long enough to consume it all, and my executors will probably have to pass much of it on to some other relative when clearing the cupboards after my death. Indeed, the rice may even become a Greenwood family heirloom.

I return to the Youth Hostel, but find myself at rather a loss as to what to do for the afternoon. It is too late in the day to begin the return journey home, which takes all day in my car. Still sad after the events of the morning, I decide to go for a walk. The obvious route is along the canal tow-path -I do seem to be spending a lot of time near canals during this trip -.in the direction of Topsham. Then I realise that I am on the wrong side of the river, as Topsham is on the opposite bank. However, all is not lost, since there is a ferry. I descend to the landing stage and peer across the river. The ferryman looks over from the Topsham bank, sees me waving, and rows across.

"How much is the fare, please?"

"60 pence. It will have to be one way, as this is the last trip of the day."

"That's fine, I'll get the bus back."

The sky is darkening as we reach the other side. As I step ashore, I ask if there is somewhere handy where I can get a cup of tea.

"You could try the Museum. That's open on a Thursday."

The rain is starting to fall as I run through the streets, rummaging in my bag for my umbrella as I go. By the time I reach the museum, rain is pouring down, bending the flowers in the gardens and driving everyone indoors. Luckily, tea is still being served, so I order a pot for one and a scone. As I drink my tea, I read a leaflet about the museum. The prize exhibit, somewhat unexpectedly, is Vivien Leigh's nightgown, the one she wore in the film "Gone With The Wind." Her first husband's family lived in Topsham, and owned the house now housing the museum, which explains how the nightgown arrived.

"I'm afraid we're closing soon," says the kind tea-lady, collecting my plate and cup. "You won't have time to look at very many of the exhibits and displays."

"Well, I wouldn't want to leave without seeing Vivien Leigh's nightgown. Where is it, please?"

"Upstairs – you'll just have time if you go now."

I dash past all the other interesting exhibits until I reach the nightgown, housed in its glass case, and with a still picture from the film showing Vivien Leigh wearing it. I have always had great admiration for Scarlett O'Hara, since receiving a copy of "Gone With The Wind" as a school prize at age fourteen. Scarlet and I were completely unalike – she a southern belle with a seventeen inch waist and a host of admirers, me a plump, studious child with knee socks and a bicycle. But she rose to the challenge presented by the hardships of the American Civil War in a multitude of ways, and who cannot but admire her for resourcefully cutting up the curtains to make a new dress when Rhett Butler was about to pay a call? In an attempt to copy her, I once altered a floral bedspread to make a hippie-type skirt, although Dotey was none too pleased, as I recall. And I adopted Scarlett's "Tomorrow is another day" as my own motto, since who knows what may be just around the corner? (In my case, preferably not any more old boyfriends, as that would be rather too unsettling.) I must have read "Gone With The Wind" and seen the film at least three times each. I stare, enthralled, at the nightgown, until a curator comes and switches off the light.

"Oh, I'm sorry, I did not realise that there was anyone still in here."

"No, I'm sorry, I've stayed past your closing time. I'll go now."

I leave the museum, and am pleased to find that the rain has stopped and the sky is brightening. I walk by the Estuary, along the Goatwalk, although I encounter no goats. Eventually, I reach a small wooden structure, just as the rain comes on again. Well, that's fine, I can shelter in this bird hide.

A woman in the bird hide looks up as I enter. "There's nothing to see here," she announces. "The rain must have put them off."

"It's OK, I really just came in to shelter."

"Same here; well, actually, I'm waiting for my husband, he's gone to B and Q."

I gaze out at the estuarine ponds, dank and bird-less, without even the odd Slovenian grebe in sight. Meanwhile, my companion has embarked upon her life story, telling me that she and her husband have retired here, although she finds the Devonian people stand-offish and less friendly than in Staffordshire.

"Sorry, I'm a Devonian."

"Well, you don't sound at all like one," in accusatory tones.

"I've been in living in Yorkshire for many years."

"Oh, that explains it! They're friendly up there, aren't they?"

"Yes, of course; but now you come to mention it, when I first went there I mistook their friendliness and thought they were rather nosey, as I was used to Devon ways. They can perhaps be rather more reticent down here."

"Well, I don't think I'll ever get used to them," complains the lady.

I am by now praying for the rain to stop, so I can make my escape, or for her husband to return from B and Q. I thought people went to bird hides to be quiet and watch birds, not to inflict their life histories onto complete strangers. That's something about being single; I've noticed that people are emboldened to talk to you, as they imagine you will be glad of their conversation, whereas if you are part of a couple, people are less inclined to approach you, since they know you have the company of your other half, a defence against intruders into coupledom, a barrier set against the idle chit-chat of the single. This present case is simply the latest example of something which has happened to me time without number, and if I am honest, I'm sure I must have done it myself. Sometimes the people are very pleasant and interesting, but often, as now, they are simply rather tedious.

"You down here on holiday then?" persists my interlocutor.

"No; for a funeral. It was this morning." That should hopefully shut her up.

"Oh." Silence. "Was it a close relative?"

Oh please. Doesn't she think that question might be a little indelicate? That she might be intruding into private grief? Remind me not to visit Staffordshire in a hurry. I remain silent, looking out onto the wet landscape, where the rain shows no sign of letting up. She can think I am another standoffish Devonian if she likes. Actually, it seems quite wet in here, my sleeve is damp, perhaps the roof is leaking. Suddenly, I realise that I am crying and my sleeve is wet with tears. Of course, this really does have the effect of silencing my companion, as no-one likes to have to deal with someone in obvious distress when all they want is a chat to while away the time until their spouse reappears after a visit to the DIY store.

The door opens and a man enters. I assume it is the long-lost husband, and that deliverance is at hand, but it is simply someone looking for birds. He glances towards the estuary and shakes his head.

"They must be feeding further down. They'll be back at high water I reckon." He makes as if to leave.

"Wait! Are you returning to civilization?"

"I'm off back to Exeter. Why, do you want a lift?"

"Yes please, to Countess Wear would be great."

"And how about you?" he asks the other lady.

"No, thanks, got to wait for my hubby…"

I reckon he must have had time to buy up everything in B and Q, or maybe he's simply decided to return to Staffordshire. Anyway, I can finally escape. I jump into my saviour's Renault, reflecting that this being rescued by strange men from remote places is becoming quite a habit, what with the Mercedes man from the country park and now this Devonian twitcher. He lets me out of the car at the traffic lights, and I run across the park to the Youth Hostel, where I find that the French party has left and all is quiet. I pack my rucksack and load the car ready for the journey home.

Chapter 52

Hamish is visiting, seeking sanctuary from the sorry state of affairs which his domestic life in Doncaster has become. Their house is full of elaborate bouquets tied with coloured ribbons, sent by Louisa's Canadian swain. He is more or less the same age as Hamish, but apparently runs marathons and has a family of native American Indians living rent-free in his attic, whereas Hamish suffers with poor health and has piles of old newspapers in the loft. Louisa is still determined to meet her internet lover as soon as possible, with a view to possibly emigrating if they still love each other once they have actually met in the flesh rather than only in a chat-room.

 "And this is a woman who gets homesick when she goes to the supermarket," fulminates Hamish. "She tells me she has never felt so loved as she is by this man; but I've loved her, even while underneath her car in the freezing road mending it yet again, even when rewiring the kitchen, and what about giving up work to be a house-husband and bring up her child, surely to goodness that's love? I've loved her for twenty years! But this chap has only to send sweet nothings over the airwaves, and that's the end for Louisa and me! And then there's the little matter of his wife - what's he going to do about her?"

I feel desperately sorry for Hamish but there is little I can say or do to help. All the same, I have to try.

"That's really not something you can do anything about. You must look after yourself, allow yourself time to grieve, then meet new people, develop new interests. I know it's hard, remember I felt terrible when Robin ditched me to go off with Tebogo in Botswana, and we had not been together anything like as long as you and Louisa have."

"But who's going to want to take up with an old codger like me? I'm over 60."

"Hamish, believe me, someone will. Look at Robin, he's almost your age, and now he's got Agnes. James Habergham - he's the same age, and he seems to have gone off with Claire – they were last seen together disappearing into the bar at that Evelyn Glennie concert and I haven't heard from either of them since, they don't return my messages; the point is, men always get a new partner, because they are in short supply. It's us women who have problems, once we are over forty, and definitely when over fifty. The statistics are against us. That's why I don't bother any more. It's not worth the time and energy and risking disappointment and people being horrid to you – do you remember that pen-friend from the Yemen who

175

told me that the 'reality didn't match the illusion' when we finally met?'"

"Yes, you told me about him; that was awful. But I'm not sure of the best place to go to meet new people – not in Doncaster, anyway."

"Evening classes, clubs, hobbies; re-join political groups. Didn't you and Louisa meet through CND?"

"No, at friend's; but we were both members of different branches of CND as it happened. And of course, that's how I met you Jess, didn't I."

Hamish sits and plays my mother's piano; he is an accomplished pianist. Soon the house resounds to the strains of Chopin, Beethoven and Brahms.

"Just volunteer to play the piano for the community singing at some over-sixties clubs and you'll soon be fighting the women off," I tell him.

John Peters writes informing me that he has sorted out Auntie Phyl's estate and that she has left me a small bequest. The enclosed cheque is for £1,000. £1,000! That's more like a small fortune. I decide to spend it on renovating the kitchen, which currently boasts tatty brown lino and shabby green wall-paper. Perhaps I can get a few new units as well, that would be good. I start to plan an expedition to B and Q, and then the phone rings. It is my friend Sehlile in Zimbabwe, telling me she needs to leave the country as soon as possible.

Of course, it is an easy decision to make, for what are a few new cupboards and floor tiles compared with an imminent threat to a friend's life? I tell her I will buy an air ticket for her to collect in Harare; it is all arranged by tea-time. She will arrive at Gatwick at the end of the month, and I will go to meet her.

"But where are you going to put her?" asks Frank. "Your house is so small."

"We'll manage somehow. Nick can go and stay with his mother for a while, and Sehlile can have his room. Asylum seekers get allocated accommodation anyway, so it will only be temporary."

"Really, Jess, what with young offenders, stray dogs, cuckolded husbands, returning ex-patriots, Scottish girl-friends, and now refugees, your home's not your own..."

"I don't see that I have any choice. I always want to help my friends. And you were glad enough to stay with me before your mother went into hospital, when she was driving you up the wall."

"Yes, I suppose that's true. But I'm fine now I have the house to myself."

"How is your mother, anyway?" Frank makes a face and shakes his head.

"She'll probably have to go into a Nursing Home when she's discharged."

"So won't the council make you sell the house to pay her care fees?"

"I suppose so; and then I'll be homeless! Didn't you tell me you were thinking of getting that little attic box-room done out? After all you've just said that you like to help your friends, haven't you Jess..."

I shake my head firmly, until I realise with relief that Frank is only joking.

Chapter 53

I walk with Mash to Hebden Bridge, where there is to be a concert in the park. She still pulls at her lead, and as she is getting so strong now, I am dragged along in her wake. Coming round a corner, I encounter a Big Issue salesman, also with a Staffordshire Bull terrier, evidently a male. His dog's lead and Mash's become entangled, and we have to stop to sort them out.

"What a lovely dog! How old is she?"

"Just a few months."

"Well, she'd be just the thing for my Rag here. Will you let me know when you want her to be mated, cos I'm after a good-looking bitch to have Rag's pups."

Rag is a stout, unprepossessing dog, with blood-shot eyes, and I have no intention of letting pretty little Mash anywhere near him. (Although I do realise that I am being lookist now.)

"She's not even had her first season yet, and anyway, I'm not sure I could cope with pups. I may get her spayed."

"Oh, that's a pity. You'd make a pot of money on the pups, they'd all sell."

I now begin to wonder if this was perhaps another reason Alex wanted a dog, as an investment. Mash is barking loudly, and looking up, I catch a glimpse Alex himself disappearing down a side street with a couple of lads wearing ragged vests, combat trousers and with spiky hair-dos. Mash strains at her leash at the sight of her master, and recognising her bark he glances back. Some sort of furtive transaction takes place, then Alex saunters over to us.

"Hi, Mum; hi Mash; here for the concert? Wouldn't have thought it was your sort of thing."

"Alex, who are those lads?"

"They're just friends of mine…"

"Really? What are their names?"

"Oh, Tez, and, um, I'm not sure what his friend is called. What's it to you?"

"Don't think I don't know what's going on! You've broken your promise to me."

"What promise? Mum, you're paranoid! Anyway, don't let's have this conversation in the street. What were you doing with that 'G Issue salesman?"

"He wants Mash to be the mother of his dog's puppies." Alex seems quite thrilled at this idea, but I resolve to have Mash spayed as soon as possible.

Alex is doing odd gardening jobs during the summer holidays, but he never seems to have much money. The Youth Club is of course closed for six weeks and, without the steadying influence of Ian and his staff, I feel that Alex may have reverted to his old druggie ways. He swears to me he has not, but he always did tell me he was not using drugs even when it was clear that he was. There has been a recent resurgence in the number of unexplained late night phone calls, after which he often has to go out briefly at odd hours. The realization dawns on me that Alex may be dealing. He is spending his gardening money on weed and selling it on.

"Alex, are you dealing in cannabis?"

"Honestly Mum, your vivid imagination! I've told you, I'm clean."

"Why do you often go out for ten minutes or so in the evenings?"

"Just to get some fresh air…and to give the dog some exercise."

The dog, perfect cover for late-night sauntering. I still have my suspicions.

I cannot let the matter rest. I feel fairly sure Alex is dealing, and fear that he will be arrested, especially if he conducts his business in the street. At home, I raise the subject again.

"Alex, you're sixteen now, and old enough to get a job and pay tax. I'm not going to have you under my roof if you are dealing or using cannabis."

"So what if I am? At least it's only weed, which is less than what I was doing last time you threw me out, and it makes my gardening money go further."

"Oh, you idiot! And what else was going on before?"

"E, Charlie, booze - anything I could get my hands on- except smack. I never took smack, 'cos those smack-heads, they're in a right mess."

"And I was ill with worry then, even not knowing the half of it! Ecstacy! Cocaine! Do you want me to be ill again, so I'll have no choice but to throw you out again, for the sake of my own sanity?"

"Well, Mum, whatever I do or don't do isn't really gong to make much difference to you, is it? You can't blame me for your sad life."

"Your life will be a even sadder, and a lot shorter, if you go through it dope- fuddled and drink-fuelled."

"Well, at least I'll have had a good time before I die."

"Hasn't it occurred to you that there are other ways of having a good time?"

"Yeah, like you did, you mean. Pissing about in canoes, bloody bird-watching, baby-sitting, hanging about in libraries, and delivering poxy parish magazines. What shit! Look at you, Mum, what are you now, nearly fifty? Your life's almost over, and what have you done with it? What have you achieved? "

The well-known teenage diversionary tactic - criticise your parents and belittle their achievements. I'm not falling for that old trick.

180

"This discussion isn't about me, Alex; you're just trying to shift the focus away from your wrong-doing. But since you ask, I did get the best O level results in the school, whereas you won't have passed any of your GCSEs, I imagine."

" I don't give a flying fart; what do I want with fucking GCSEs?"

"Language! They help you get a better job."

"I bet I can make more dealing than you do working at Nick's advice centre."

"Until of course you get caught and charged, when you might find that you need Nick's help if you want to avoid being sent to prison."

"Won't get sent down for a first offence."

"That's only what you hope! It depends on what the magistrates think. And anyway, why run the risk?"

"OK, Mum, how about this -. I won't need to do anything to upset you if you let me have some of that money Auntie Phyl left you."

"You know most of that's gone to buy Sehlile a ticket to get out of Zimbabwe."

"You'd rather spend money on some African woman than on your own son!"

"My son is wilfully choosing to behave like an idiot, whereas Sehlile is a sensible, hard-working young woman whom I've known for several years, who has the misfortune to be living in a country where people are illegally being imprisoned and tortured! " By this time, I am shrieking.

Alex looks rather taken aback. "Hmm. that's true I suppose. And she did help you when Nick and I went missing. Have you let her have all the money?"

"No, there is some still left. Alex, if you mend your ways and start behaving in a manner which merits it, I might – only might - consider lending it to you."

"What - only lend?"

"Yes; you can pay me back, just as Tom is doing. But he was at university and had an overdraft. What exactly do you want money for, apart from the usual?"

"I want to take Lorna to Blackpool to see the lights sometime this autumn."

"OK. That seems like a good thing to be thinking about. I'll draw up a list of tasks you can do for me before I decide whether to let you have any money. And another thing, you'd save money if you gave up smoking. Why don't you try those patches? You can get them free while you're under eighteen."

Alex agrees to try. Next morning, I present him with a list of chores. These include washing and valeting the car, Hoovering throughout the house, sweeping the yard, clearing out the cellar, picking blackberries and washing the twenty seven jam-jars I have found so far. I have also made him a doctor's appointment to get the nicotine patches, so he can make a start on giving up smoking. Alex finds it hard to hide his contempt.

"Clearing the cellar? So you can fill it up with more junk? And picking pissing blackberries! Enough to fill **twenty-seven** jars?"

"Jelly, and you're usually glad enough to eat it."

"Come to think of it – can't you make wine with blackberries? And are those old demijohns still in the cellar? Mum, you might be onto something after all."

Chapter 54

Sehlile is arriving on the overnight flight from Zimbabwe and I go down on the coach to Gatwick, to meet her and bring her back to Yorkshire. She wants to study in Leeds, where she has relatives. We are both too tired to talk much, and since the ventilation system is not working, conditions on the coach are extremely uncomfortable, but still, it is lovely to see her again. I tell her she will not recognise Alex, no longer the cute twelve-year old she remembers.
I do not want to ask her about life in Zimbabwe at the moment, as it must be painful for her to have to leave her native country under the present difficult circumstances. Other members of her large extended family are still there, facing daily hardship, and possibly much worse. I am so relieved that she has been able to get away.

Like many Africans, used to living in countries where rabies is endemic, Sehlile is not keen on dogs, which disappoints Mash, who always wants to give new arrivals a rapturous welcome. Sehlile says she thinks Yorkshire is beautiful, but I remind her she will require lots of warm clothes once summer is over. We look in the local charity shops and stock up with several jumpers.

Sehlile reads my short stories, and says she likes them. I have also had an encouraging response from other friends who have looked at them, and people have asked me why I don't try to get them published. I know it is very hard for a first time author to get into print, and have been looking into the possibility of bringing out the collection myself, although the cost of printing turns out to be more than I can afford. Then David, my Piscean friend, suggests Berringden Books, a small local publishing house, which might perhaps be interested in taking my stories. I ring and speak to the man who runs Berringden Books, but he does not sound very hopeful, explaining that they receive a lot of unsolicited material, but have to be fairly sure of recovering their costs before they can accept a manuscript for publication. However, as I live quite close, I can drop it in the next time I am in town. I leave the folder containing my "Stories of love and misunderstanding" on the table, having been warned that everyone is very busy and I should not expect to hear anything for some time.

Meanwhile, Alex's bike has been stolen from outside the house where he has been gardening, despite having a strong padlock. I suppose thieves go about with hacksaws tucked up their jumpers these days. Alex rings me, asking me to come and fetch him, as he is stranded in Berringden Green, supposedly one of the better areas of the town. I put Mash in the car, as she enjoys a ride, and set off to collect him. I am driving back towards Berringden Brow, when I spot a teenage lad and girl wheeling a bike along the road.

"Look, Alex! Isn't that your bike?"

"Fuck, that's my bike!"

I bring the car to a rapid halt, and leap out to confront the astonished couple.

"That's my son's bike!"

"Whadya on about? I just borrowed it off me mate!"

By this time, I have wrested the bike from the lad's grasp and am loading it into the back of the car.

"Ere, you can't just go round snatching people's bikes off them!" he protests.

"I can if it's my lad's bike, which it is. And if you try to stop me I'll get the dog." Any empty threat, as of course little Mash would only lick him to death.

"What's me mate gonna say when I tell 'im some old biddy snatched 'is bike?"

"He'll know it's a fair cop, as someone stole this bike this afternoon. They've even sawn through the padlock. What's your mate's name?"

"Jason. And what's yours?"

"Jess, this is my mobile number, and I'm a magistrate. Any queries and he can discuss them with me."

Alex and Mash are watching, amazed, from the car window. I am glad Alex does not speak up to say that I am **not** a magistrate, as of course I have lied about this. Indeed, Alex appears to be almost lost for words, managing only the occasional "Fuck me!"

Unsurprisingly, Jason never rings.

Chapter 55

Two days later, I am surprised to receive a call from Berringden Books, asking me when I can come in and talk about my manuscript, with a view to early publication. It seems that their chief reader came in, picked up my folder from the desk, and began idly flicking through it. Her partner heard the sound of laughter, and came out of the next room to see what she was finding so amusing. He then began reading the stories and also liked them. I am in luck.

What with this flurry of excitement over fetching Sehlile from the airport and placing the stories, I have had no time to go to the library. When I eventually get there, much to my surprise I find that Ben greets me like a long-lost friend.

"There you are! I thought you must have dropped off the face of the planet!"

"I've actually been quite busy, having meetings with my publishers..."

"Publishers! Ah, you must mean a **Vanity** house." Ben, clearly amazed at my news, has emerged from behind the counter, and is dancing round me as I make my way towards to the reference section. It is a long time since I have seen Ben behaving in such an animated fashion, and I am pleased to observe that

185

he has apparently left his mid-life crisis, (if indeed that is what it was), behind him.

"No, go wash your mouth out with soap and water! I mean Berringden Books."

"Berringden Books! Really? So you don't have to pay anything? They pay?"

"Exactly so." I sweep upstairs, as the astonished Ben returns to the counter.

There is a programme on television about young people looking for lost parents. They have employed someone to help, a 'people finding expert.' I idly wonder whether this is really necessary, surely all that needs to be done to start a search is to type the person's name into the internet and see what comes up. Then I have the idea of trying to trace Alex's absent father, Roger the oceanographer; after all, as an academic he would hardly be inclined to hide his light under a bushel. I type his name into the computer and dozens of references appear. He seems to have had a good career, as there are conference reports and workshop papers from all over the world. However, he is now back, working at the same laboratory as when I knew him, and his email address and work telephone number are both listed. A photo appears, of Roger and his oceanographic colleagues. I note that his hair has receded, whereas Bill, Tom's father, still has a full head of hair. Alex presently has lovely thick dark hair, and it will be a shame if he loses it, but there is as yet no cure for inherited male pattern baldness, so far as I know.

I call Alex upstairs and tell him the news. He lies on the bed, playing with the dog, as I read through the list of his illustrious father's academic publications.

"A two dimensional slice model of the shelf edge region off the West coast of Scotland – a model response to realistic seasonal forcing and the role of the M2 tide."

"Numerical investigation into the effect of freshwater inputs on the circulation in Pelous Sound, New Zealand."

"A coastal ocean model inter-comparison study for a three dimension idealised test case."

"Development of portable shelf sea models for massively parallel machines."

Alex is looking distinctly unimpressed. "I've only known this bloke for five minutes and already I'm bored with him."

Mash scrabbles at the door, asking to be let out. "Come on Mash, walkies."

Unlike the young people featured on the father-finding television programme, willing to travel the country or even the world to find their fathers, Alex seems content to go no further than the intenet, sensibly preferring to spend time playing with a loyal pup rather than chasing after an irrelevant absent father.

Chapter 56

Frank comes over for a Barn Dance and finds me correcting proofs for my "Stories of Love and Misunderstanding." I have not yet told him about their imminent publication.

"Oh, still working on those stories – you'll never finish them."

"Actually, I have."

"Well, you'll never find a publisher."

"Berringden Books have taken them."

"Oh. Of course, they're only a **micro** publisher. You won't sell many."

"People are already ordering them for Christmas presents."

For Frank of course, the glass is always half empty; but, refusing to let his lack of enthusiasm discourage me, I am presently going round with a happy smile, which lasts until we receive Alex's exam results. They are predictably bad, with nothing higher than Grade D. This of course wipes the grin off my face. However, despite this poor showing, he manages to blag his way onto a photography course at the local college, by passing a basic literacy test. I am pleased and relieved, although rather surprised at his choice; but as he explains, he enjoyed taking photos of the animals and birds when we were in Africa. I smile as I recall those pictures, usually of empty patches of bush from which the creature had just flown or run away as the shot was being taken. He will enjoy learning how to do it properly.

Berringden Books is planning a launch party for my "Stories of Love and Misunderstanding" at the weekend. Lorna is again staying here with Alex, Tom and Rose have travelled up from Bristol, Hamish is coming over from Doncaster, Sehlile has arrived from Leeds, and Nick is once more in residence, so the house is full. However, I have long since ceased worrying about where to put everyone, I just give everyone bedrolls and blankets and tell them to find a congenial piece of floor-space. There is quite a queue for the bathroom in the morning, though, and we do get through large quantities of tea, toast, breakfast cereal and pasta, although strangely enough, no-one seems to want to partake of Auntie Phyl's brown rice bequest.

As well as all the houseguests, lots of people are coming for the afternoon, including Tom's father Bill and his partner Chris, Robin and his friend Charlie, David, Pete and their partners, plus the rest of my fellow Pisceans, Jim the vicar, and several of my old friends from university days. Frank has declined an invitation, since he has to visit Mother, (still in hospital, and giving cause for concern), and Ben also sends his apologies, saying that he has to rewire his house that very day.

I am rather nervous at the idea of having to read in front of such a large audience, but as I look up and see the happy faces smiling encouragingly at me, I realise that I am among friends, and the realisation gives me confidence. The reading is well received, and immediately afterwards Tom and Alex come over to tell me how proud they are – at least, Tom tells me while Alex nods - which means a great deal to me. I am nearly fifty, and despite what Alex may think, my life so far has been full. I have two fine sons, two degrees, for what they are worth, lots of friends, and now I've written a book. Middle age can be fun after all, once the crises have been dealt with, and I seem to have been dealing with rather a lot lately, my own and other peoples', what with Alex's teenage tantrums, drug dealings, the aftermath of Nick's madcap overseas adventures, Hamish's heartache over Louisa and the internet lover, Robin's unexpected and unsettling return from Africa, Frank's strange Valentine's day tricks, followed by the worries over his mother's declining health, Sehlile's precipitate flight from the horrors of Zimbabwe, Auntie Phyl's death, and Gilbert Brown's inappropriate harking back to the days of lost youth, not to mention that unpleasantness over the clematis, and the stress of moving house, now all thankfully behind me.

Next, I have the thrill of signing the first few copies of my stories for people who want to buy them, followed by something of a come-down, since the publishers have asked to make the tea. A writer's work is never done...

I have planned a trip to Blackpool, for Tom and Alex, both the girlfriends, Sehlile, Nick and the dog, so that we can show Lorna the lights, and Sehlile and Mash can see the sea for the first time. Mash capers about on the sand, wild with excitement. I run after her, trying to entice her back to me with a stick – all this exercise is definitely doing me good. I realise that I am becoming quite dotty about the dog; I know she won't let me down, as a man might do, Mash does not mind my greying hair, her needs are simple and consistent and she won't play tricks or hurt me. She will not be critical or disparaging, indeed, she thinks I am wonderful. She is good company, and when I start taking her to obedience training classes later this autumn we will make lots of new friends, both human and canine.

We all eat fish and chips, admire the lights, and then climb wearily onto the train home. Mash receives a second marriage proposal, from a man in Accrington, on behalf of his dog Gnasher, a male Staffie named after the Beano character, canine companion of Dennis the Menace. We pass the journey choosing possible names for any future offspring of Mash and Gnasher, and come up with Bash, Crash, Dash, Rash, Lash, Sash, Gash, and Alex's particular favourite, Hash. Of course, like any protective mother, I am not going to let Mash start courting yet, as she's still only a pup.

Next day, Tom and Rose return to Bristol by train, Alex goes by coach to Scotland with Lorna for half term, Sehlile returns to Leeds and Nick decides to visit his mother. It is a fine day, so Mash and I go out blackberry picking, and quickly gather seven pounds (at least, I pick that amount and Mash eats the ones I drop.) We return home at teatime. Everyone has gone, no sons or lodgers are in residence, and the house is quiet at last.

Also by Jill Robinson:

Berringden Brow – Memoirs of a Single Parent with a Crush

Meet Jess and her friends, the struggling but still optimistic middle-aged women of Berringden Brow.

Good degrees, poor employment prospects, coping with bizarre job interviews, stroppy teenage kids, ageism, sexism, lookism, sizeism… scanning the personal columns in search of a rare eligible man **without** hypochondria, a live-in mother, multiple allergies, a preference for playing with toy soldiers, the inability to keep a date, or a penchant for sex in public places.

But whenever it all gets too much for Jess, she can always escape into the library…

"…this richly enjoyable, funny and humane read."
Sue Limb.

Available from good bookshops or by visiting www.penninepens.co.uk

Email: jill@berringdenbrow.co.uk